When Love Comes Knocking

A Journey of Happiness and Heartaches, Break-ups, and Breakthroughs

LaWanda Lewis Burrell

SUSU Entertainment LLC
P.O. Box 1621
Cypress, TX 77410
susuentertainmentllc.com

Printed in the United States of America
Library of Congress Cataloging-in-Publication Data

Name: LaWanda Lewis Burrell, Author

Title: When Love Comes Knocking | Subtitle: A Journey of Happiness and Heartaches, Break-ups and Breakthroughs | Summary: A journey of complicated situations of love that requires you to put forth a lot of patience and understanding. You will have to decide if the issues will keep you together or break you apart.

Identifiers:
ISBN: 978-1-956292-09-1 (paperback)
ISBN: 978-1-956292-08-4 (hardcover)
ISBN: 978-1-956292-20-6 (e-book)

Subjects: Fiction | Relationships | Your Marriage Is What You Make It | Single and Alone Doesn't Mean Lonely | Love Yourself First | Prayer and Patience | Choose Happiness

Book Cover Design © 2022 by SUSU Entertainment LLC

Table of Contents

Introduction

Are you a fan of reality shows, soap operas or TV dramas? Do you enjoy cuddling up on the sofa streaming your favorite movies, documentaries, TV series, or binge-watching high-profile shows? Have you ever fallen in love, out of love, or just afraid to love? You will enjoy these gripping stories that will take you on a journey of happiness and heartaches, break-ups, and breakthroughs.

You may go through trials that may disturb your peace and test your faith. The situation may knock you down, but you will learn to get back up again. In these stories, you will find that your struggles may become your strength to give you the power to forgive and allow your bitterness to turn into your better-ness. In these complicated relationships, you will have to decide if the love is strong enough to hang in there for the long haul or throw in the towel. "When Love Comes Knocking, will you answer?"

Chapter 1

Focus On Loving Yourself First

People keep telling you over and over again that the right person will come along. You have been dating and waiting for years and you feel that your future spouse has entered another planet, got hit by a bus or just changed his or her mind. You are among millions that are ready to hang up the dating scene and find true love. Everyone around you has been getting engaged, married, and having babies. Every year your birthday comes around and your biological clock is ticking and ticking, not even having a prospect to date.

Although some guys are dealing with the same thing, looking for that special someone, it is more common for women to become discouraged, because they are truly ready for love. Not only are you getting pressured from your girlfriends and co-workers, your parents and grandparents ask you about getting married every time you come home to visit. You enjoy your quality time, and your career means the world to you, but you are ready to settle down and have babies with the love of your life.

What is keeping you single? Is it that your standards are too high or too low? Are you stuck in your ways? Trust issues? Self-esteem issues? Daddy issues? Too busy, being busy? Is your pride getting in the way? Are you always choosing the same type? Have your past relationships created so much hurt that it is too difficult to move forward? Did you have compatibility issues, lack of forgiveness, or the relationship was not a priority and there were scheduling conflicts?

These are all valid reasons, but can you admit that it just may be you? Your big ego may be getting in the way of love. Remember you can't get different results always having the same mindset. Change it up a bit and get outside of your comfort zone. Maybe the last relationship didn't work out because of bad timing, or they reminded you of someone else.

Maybe you didn't feel worthy because of generational curses of unsuccessful relationships within your family, or you're a homebody and never get out to meet anyone. How can your special someone find you if you're always stuck between those four walls? I know you are tired of dancing with your own shadows. However, if you are single and alone it doesn't necessarily mean that you are lonely. Having a single life has its advantages. You can be more creative, and you don't have to compromise. You have more quality time to understand your likes and dislikes. You can travel, shop on a whim, and have more flexibility and freedom to accomplish your goals.

When you are single you are stressed less, self-care is your priority, and you have more time with friends. Although being married is a beautiful thing, especially when it is with the right person, never make decisions by force. Your single life is what you make it. Always choose happiness because this is your life to live. Do not give up pieces of yourself for anyone. Do not accept a version of your life that you are not truly happy with, or you may one day surrender to regret.

Lack of forgiveness plays a huge part in not being able to move forward and experience true agape love. You are constantly making everyone you meet pay for the pain and hurt endured by your ex. Forgiveness doesn't take the hurt away, but it allows you to move forward to make room for the blessings that God has for you. Living a life of un-forgiveness may keep you single or will keep your relationship stagnant, which may lead to one partner seeking excitement elsewhere.

Unfortunately, we must face the realization that marriage is not for everyone. God gives the gift of the single life to some, and the gift of married life to others. Some people come in your life for a reason, and some only come for a season. Don't be discouraged. I am not a relationship expert, but I have had my share of love and compassion, heartaches, and pain. Love is a beautiful thing but being in a relationship takes a lot of trust, love, understanding, compromise, and willingness to forgive.

You cannot give up on someone because the situation is not ideal, because good relationships aren't good because there are no problems, they are good because both of you care enough about the relationship to try and make it work. Let's look at your life and we will analyze some things to help you get closer to the blessings that God has for you.

Check your heart. It is important to take a self-evaluation. Does your heart beat with love and kindness, loyalty, and respect? We must constantly work on ourselves before we will be blessed with the desires of our heart. You can't make yourself happy by bringing misery to other people. It will only lead to a disastrous and unhappy life. Marriage is a lifelong commitment, and you have been told that you have some selfish ways. Always show respect and appreciation for one another. A healthy marriage is when yesterday's disagreement doesn't ruin today's communication. Sometimes it is ok to agree to disagree. In a marriage, it is not your way or the highway, use your differences and make them your strength.

Marriage is about sharing. It will no longer be mine, but ours. Are you ready to give up your free-spirited lifestyle? What about the shopping sprees whenever it is convenient for you? Out of respect for your partner, big purchases should be discussed and agreed upon. Don't forget about the weekend getaways with your single girlfriends or the fellas. You may be able to continue with some of your same routines if you communicate and keep an open mindset. Allowing your partner to have their alone time is very important, whether it is watching TV in a different room, reading a book in the backyard, taking a walk by yourself, visit with a homeboy or girlfriend, or doing some window shopping, having a quick break from your partner is necessary. As the saying goes, "Absence makes the heart grow fonder." Ultimately, praying together, loving one another, and spending quality time will help you have a happy and healthy marriage.

Effective communication is the key prior to walking down the aisle of commitment. In a serious relationship, it is important to visualize you and your significant other together forever. However, can you deal with them and their baggage? Know your limits, what is a deal breaker for you? If you don't like long distance relationships, because of mistrust from your past exes, then don't re-visit the same situation, but remember everybody is different. Having a friendship first and truly liking your mate is very important, because it takes the stress from some of the things that you may not have any control over. You are not perfect, so don't expect perfection from your mate. Although some situations may not be relevant until after you are married, always remember to discuss as much as you can prior to saying, "I Do."

In **Genesis 1:28,** And God blessed them, and God said unto them, "Be fruitful, and multiply, and replenish the earth, and subdue it: and have dominion over the fish of the sea, and over the fowl of the air, and over every living thing that moveth upon the earth." Have you discussed having children? Everybody that enters the covenant of marriage doesn't necessarily want children. If you want children, how many? What if you can't conceive? Will you consider other alternatives? Does he or she have children from a previous relationship? If you were raised with a different religious background, how will you raise your children?

Will both of you work outside the home? Finances are the leading causes of stress in a relationship, and it contributes to at least 50% of the reasons marriages fail. Don't wait, talk about it now. Will you have joint bank accounts or separate? Does he or she have a good credit score? Have you discussed household debt? Are you looking into home ownership, or renting? Does he or she have a bad habit that you can't ignore? These are questions that you must ask yourself when considering a lifetime of forever's with the one you love.

Are you that angry person that is never able to be approached? You wear a mask of fear everywhere you go. You can't enjoy your life because you are always thinking the worst. You carry worry, hurt and disappointment on your shoulders, which is reflected in your facial expressions. Smile! Let the world know behind the tough demeanor, you are a nice person. Learn to take control of your emotions, don't let them control you. You cannot overcome what you can't confront. Stop projecting your pain on others. There may be things in your life that need fixing. Learn to pray and get aligned with the Most High God. You deserve a new and rejuvenated life to call your own.

Learn to love yourself first. You must know how to treat yourself before you can expect anyone else to treat you like a king or queen. Think about the things in life that brings you joy. Life doesn't stop just because you are not where you would like to be. Enjoy your moment in the now. Life is short and tomorrow isn't promised to you. Know that you are beautiful and worthy of having a good life. If that relationship didn't work out, it is ok. God has other plans for you that is better than before. Keep the faith and know that you will get your happiness back again. Don't ruin your character and compare your life to others. Some of us struggle with this daily. Envy can lead you into a life of destruction and not allow you to see the beauty of Christ. Jealousy is a form of hatred built upon insecurities. Always be happy to see others doing well and finding their true love, because yours may be right around the corner. Be patient and enjoy your quality time. Use your alone time to get a closer relationship with God, understand who you truly are, and refine your character.

Ladies, we can be very animated, spontaneous, and full of ourselves. Some guys are attracted to those characteristics, but make sure it is not overkill. We don't always have to get the last word or prove our points with dramatic gestures. Most guys like a peaceful and drama free home. His home is his castle, and if he can't chill and enjoy quiet time there, he will definitely find it somewhere else. I remember Mama would say, "Pick your battles." While we are free to choose our actions, we aren't free to choose the consequences of our actions.

Negativity doesn't look good on anyone. Stop being a drama king or queen and talk with each other sensibly and respectfully. When you finally meet that special someone, don't be so quick to plan a wedding as soon as you meet, because you are setting yourself up to be hurt. Love yourself enough to know that it is ok to enjoy spending time by yourself. You are wonderfully and fearfully made by God, although it is great to have a companion, you don't need anyone else to complete you.

God's timing is the best. Our timing is not always God's timing. If you are not married it could mean that you should just be patient and wait. Maybe God is preparing you to be at your best for your companion who is better than the rest. Your prince charming may not be ready to receive his goddess, he may be battling with struggles that God wants to mend before placing him or her in your path. Trust that blessings are manifested in God's perfect timing. This is very hard for most women because we are planners. We want to be in control of our lives. If it takes too long to find someone, we may decide to take our exes back. Never go back for less because you are too impatient to wait for the best. The minute you do that, you may end up getting lesser than what you want to settle for. Always know the difference between what you are getting and what you deserve.

We must understand that it doesn't matter how many blind dates you go on, speed dating services you participate in, or online dating sites you register with, your lifelong partner won't find you until God says it is time. You don't need validation from anyone to make you happy. As a single woman desiring to be married, I never stopped living. My favorite pastime was traveling, cooking, reading, writing, enjoying my family, going to dinner with friends, and participating in church activities.

Find a hobby, enjoy a painting class, join an organization, workout at the gym, or volunteer at a nearby school or nursing home. Sometimes being in a relationship with the wrong person will hinder you from meeting the right person. I would often wonder when God would spread the blessings of love my way, but I knew everything had a time and a season.

You should always have a good judgment of character. Guys, you visualize having a virtuous woman, someone to take home to Mama. Well maybe check the places you are going to find your future companion. Going to the strip clubs every week isn't going to work. Your future wife probably won't be hanging on a pole. You must learn to look beyond a woman's waistline. You may not get blessed with what you want, it may be just what you need. There is no perfect man or perfect woman, but you want to pray for someone that is good to you and for you, someone you can trust and can trust you. You want to settle down, but you have been lying and cheating, which have gotten the best of you over the years. Learn to make the right choices, because no one wants to live with someone they can't trust.

Nothing good comes out of having deceitful ways. Ladies, you must follow these same guidelines. You enjoy having a guy to take you shopping, another one to take you out to dinner and a movie, a sports buddy to get you into the football and basketball games, different sex buddies, and a travel partner. Unless you are openly communicating to these guys that they are not your one and only, you will face some difficulties. Be careful with having physical contact with multiple partners because they may not protect themselves, and you are putting yourself at risk. You think having several guys will get you everything you want but understand that karma is real. What you do to others will come back to you. As you have heard growing up, "Treat people how you want to be treated."

When you are getting serious about someone, observe them in every way, talking, praying, explaining, venting, joking, laughing, and gossiping. Do they engage in meaningful conversations? Are they often speaking positively or negatively? Have they dealt with past traumas in their life? Do they love themselves? Stop ignoring the red flags. You see the signs, but you think that you will change him or her. Listen to what they say and how they respond to adversity. It can sometimes be difficult to tell if someone means well, but always keep your best interest in mind when you are looking for that special someone.

Some adults are still dealing with trust and abandonment issues from their childhood. They have been emotionally bruised and abused from a parent or guardian being unavailable, and this has damaged their relationships throughout the years. The hard truth is you must deal with your past to be healed from your past. The broken little girl or little boy has been rejected so many times from a family member that it is difficult to move forward. Not properly handling these types of issues will keep you single and destroy a marriage. Praying, forgiving, and seeking therapy from a professional is necessary.

Although you may not be where you want to be, learn to look at your life through a different lens. Do you see failure, defeat, and low self-esteem? Wipe your lens and see success, victory, and self-confidence. You are one in a million! No matter what obstacles you've had to face, or unfair cards your life dealt you, take time to forgive, let go and let God, because holding grudges will only put a halt on your blessings.

Have self-worth and don't be so desperate that you settle for anybody. Don't entertain toxic relationships, they are not good for your health. You cannot change someone who doesn't see that they have an issue. You're so busy trying to fix them, but in return it breaks you. Again, pay attention to the red flags because they may not go away but get worse. You meet a guy, and you want to trust him, but he has shown you what he is all about. You see him playing games with several different women, so what makes you think he will be different with you? Guys, you know she has a lot of baggage, and she constantly disturbs your peace, but you continue to sleep with her because you are mesmerized with her looks and body. You are playing Russian roulette with your life, don't be a sucker for love.

Change your behavior. You can change if you want to, by praying and asking God to help you become a better man or better woman. You must put in the effort to make it happen. God only helps those that help themselves. Try not to get caught up with just the physical, although it is pleasurable to the eyes, physical traits will change over a period of time. Fall in love with a woman or man's mind, body, soul, and spirit. A woman has a lot more to offer than just her *junk in her trunk*. A man has more to offer than his *money and muscles*.

Learn to get to know a person beyond the physical and material. You may be a good guy, but always seem to be caught up with high maintenance, no-good, gold-digging women. Check your surroundings, maybe you are shopping around in the wrong area of town. A relationship cannot function on looks alone. Your eyes may lead you to her but allow your ears to listen and be the deciding factor.

Men don't compartmentalize your feelings. We love men to be powerful, trustworthy, secure, confident, God-fearing, good communicators, honorable, loving, respectful, and romantic. We want you to be able to express yourself, and we should be open to listen. It is ok for you to talk about your emotions, this may eliminate you from lashing out at your partner and being stressed in the relationship. Learn to align your words with your actions. Be accountable. Don't be afraid to seek medical attention. Go to the doctor and get a regular check-up because your presence is needed in the world. Don't hide your feelings. Vulnerability can be sexy in a man; it is not a sign of weakness as you may have been taught. Your openness will help you to have productive and healthy conversations. Don't fear rejection. If you are interested in someone, let them know. Women cannot read your minds, the same way you can't read theirs. Don't miss out on an opportunity because you fear rejection. If it doesn't work out, then they weren't meant for you. Rejection isn't always bad; it just may be a blessing and save you from a lifetime of headaches. Take your time, pray and be patient, you will eventually find your queen.

Men are attracted to the physical traits first, but some women are doing too much to impress a man. Women be confident, love yourself first, and have self-worth to know that you are beautiful without a face full of makeup, unappealing weaves, wigs, and lashes, wearing tight and revealing clothing, and total body makeovers. Learn to leave some things for the man's imagination. He shouldn't see your total package until you are in a committed relationship. Be yourself and don't be desperate. You want a potential partner to love and respect you, but sometimes doing too much may run them away or attract the wrong type of companion. Ladies let's aim to be classy not trashy. A lot of men like women with natural beauty, self-confidence, someone with a good character, good conversation, goals, and aspirations. When it comes to being in a relationship, whether you are looking for your king or queen, you are the author of your story, express yourself, look the part and choose your companion wisely.

Chapter 2

What God Has for You Is for You

What God has for you is for you! You must find someone that you have a common interest with, that has a loving heart, and that will be good to you and for you. On our first date my husband, DeMorris, shared with me about his past relationships, how he had been married before, but wasn't afraid to love again. He not only wanted to find a good wife, but he also wanted to be a good husband. DeMorris had been watching me at work for many months because we worked in the same building, but for different companies. I didn't know he liked me because I didn't know he existed. He was waiting for the moment to get me alone, but I was always around my friends.

He was a good guy that suffered a lot of hardships growing up. God was waiting for me to meet him when he had made him into a new creature in Christ. We crossed each other's path when I was stressed and depressed, overworked, and underpaid. It wasn't the best time in my HR career. God wanted me to see how a real man is supposed to treat you, he wasn't there when everything was good. He saw me when I was at my lowest, unemployed, and dealing with health issues. I tried to say things to run him away, in order for me to reject him before he could reject me.

Surprisingly, he was there for me without hesitation, even when I thought he would leave, he showed me for better or worse, before walking down the aisle. I met a man of wisdom, intelligence, a great provider, handsome, funny, beautiful spirit, loved God, caring, respectful, and showed me unconditional love. My husband met me, an independent woman filled with a pure heart of love and kindness, smart, caring, funny, beautiful spirit, loved God, her family, and herself but was bruised from a previous long-term relationship. Thankfully he approached one of my friends about me, and we have been together for 18 years and happily married for 16 years with 3 beautiful children, and an older son from his previous marriage.

Be flexible when dating and be willing to open your heart to something new or you may be stuck in the same situations that you never wanted to be in. Be careful with what you share with your single friends, because some of them desire to be in a relationship and will do or say anything to not see you in one.

When my husband and I dated, I kept our progression to myself as much as I could, because everyone around you may not be happy that you have finally found true love. Your so-called friends may start to become envious and jealous of your relationship. Some of my co-workers would try and pry, occasionally asking the status of our dating. They weren't genuinely concerned about our love. They were bold enough to say to me, "Well if it doesn't work out, I will be next in line," as if my boyfriend would give them the time of day. Always remember what is meant for you is for you. No one has a perfect life but know who is truly for you.

These women were single and hungry for love. There were all types of women, ones that hadn't gotten over the hurt from a past relationship, stating that all men are dogs, cheaters, and worthless jerks. There were women that enjoyed sleeping around, thinking this would be the way Mr. Right would come knocking at their door. There were the holy rollers, only looking for the love from Jesus Christ, stating that they didn't need a man, because King Jesus gave them everything they needed.

The high maintenance women, stating that their mate needs to have a specific amount of money in his bank account, no children, a Mercedes, BMW, Porsche, or some type of luxury vehicle. Oh, and the Mama's girl, she can't seem to find a man because she is always hanging with Mama. Mama never had a good relationship because she was constantly hurt by men, and now she is throwing that same hurt to her daughter.

DeMorris told me that he was looking for a woman with not only a pretty face but a woman of substance, a virtuous woman. God had given him a second chance in life, and he was looking for a wife. Although, I thought it was very soon to have this conversation, I knew that I was dealing with a grown man that had experienced the ups and downs of life and was ready for something new. I knew that God was preparing someone for me. I decided until he comes, I would continue to live a happy life. I was raised as an independent woman; life was not always easy for me. I endured a lot of heartaches and heartbreaks, but I kept pushing. No matter how hard your life gets, or how many friends you lose along the way, you must keep doing your best. Let the haters continue to hate, use it as motivation to strive for excellence.

Remember some smiles are frowns turned upside down. True friends are hard to find, and you may have to do some spring cleaning to know who is truly for you. Stop telling all your business. Whatever goals you want to accomplish in life, just do it! You don't need validation from anyone to be successful. Don't let other's limited thinking hinder what you are capable of. Pray and go for it! While single, I wanted a successful career, so I updated my resume, applied, and interviewed for positions. I wanted to buy a house, so I checked the housing market in my area, saved my money and closed on my very first home at 24-years-old. I wanted a brand-new car, so I did my research, saved my money, and bought one. I loved to travel, so I got my passport ready and flew the friendly skies.

I wanted to have financial stability, so I saved and contributed to my company's 401K match program. Later as I gained more knowledge about financial planning, I started to invest my money. I loved to try new foods, so I cooked a nice meal for myself and enjoyed going out with friends. I loved looking good, so I pampered myself. I loved to read a good book, so I bought books, and checked out books from the library. I enjoyed writing, so I started journaling about my life. I wanted to learn a new hobby, so I took salsa lessons and swimming lessons. I wanted to be married and have children, so I prayed and waited on God. Your life shouldn't be placed on hold because you are not where you want to be. Pray, plan and work hard to get to your destiny.

Most of my friends were getting married every year. It was not always easy being the bridesmaid and never the bride. I was set up with a couple of blind dates that never seemed to work out. Before I met my husband, I went to church alone for many years, and although I had a boyfriend, he never wanted to go to church with me because he was content with watching TV church. I would often see the families making plans after church to go to dinner. I was never jealous, but I always visualized and prayed to God to have a family of my own to worship and enjoy family dinners with.

You are special and worthy of having the best life ever. When I wanted to have a pity party, I got on my knees and prayed. Whether you have a significant other or not, learn to love you! I enjoyed having a good time with me, treating myself whenever possible. Fall in love with taking care of yourself and live in your wholeness. You deserve happiness first, so don't be afraid to be alone. Remember you don't need approval from others to be liked. Be inspired and know that love will come knocking sooner than later.

Kayleigh and Audrey met at a car wash in the southwest side of Philadelphia, Pennsylvania. Their friendship soared as they found out that they were part of the same sorority. The two loved to talk on the phone, shop together, attend sorority events and enjoy Philadelphia's downtown cuisines and historic culture. Kayleigh was more outgoing than Audrey because she knew a lot of people in the city and all the fun hang out spots because she grew up there.

Audrey was originally from Natchez, Mississippi and had moved up north for job opportunities and a change of scenery. Both girls were in relationships that seemed to be heading downhill, but it didn't stop them from living their best lives. Audrey was always asked to be a bridesmaid in her friend's weddings. She was happy to be asked, but often wondered when it would be her time to be the bride. Kayleigh invited Audrey out with her and some friends. They were throwing one of their classmates a bachelorette party at a strip club. It was Audrey's first time going to a strip club. She was very conservative and felt awkward attending one of those events but didn't want to be a party pooper.

As the male dancers were introduced on the stage, the ladies yelled as they were mesmerized with their sweaty six packs, bulging muscles and sexy dance moves. The crowd went wild! Out of nowhere, the announcer asked for a volunteer to be serenaded by one of the dancers. The spotlight shined through the crowd. Kayleigh and her friends turned to Audrey and here comes the dancer picking her up and sitting her in the chair on the stage. Audrey was so nervous and in shock, all she remembered was loud screaming from her girlfriends, seeing a bed of roses and whip cream. Deep down, Audrey felt so uncomfortable and hated that they had singled her out. *Wasn't the event for the bachelorette?* Audrey wondered but decided to be a good sport and enjoy the fun. It was definitely a night her and Kayleigh won't ever forget.

Work had started to really pick up for Audrey and there was very little time to go out with Kayleigh and the girls. She was so happy that although her new position, working for a governmental agency required a lot of hard work, she had been blessed with getting a raise. It had been a while since Kayleigh had spoken with Audrey when out of the blue, she called to tell her that she had met someone special. Kayleigh described Jason as a fun, loving, older guy that loved to cook and knew what he wanted in life. They had so much in common and were really enjoying getting to know each other.

Audrey was happy for Kayleigh but stayed her distance because with the sound of Kayleigh's tone, she knew it was something very serious. One day Audrey called to speak to Kayleigh, and Jason her new boyfriend, answered the phone. He was so sweet telling Audrey that he had heard a lot about her and couldn't wait to meet her. Jason said that Kayleigh was at the grocery store getting items because he was cooking dinner. He asked, "What are you eating for dinner?" Audrey chuckled, and said, "Honey Nut Cheerios." Jason asked her to come and eat dinner with them so that she could eat a real meal.

Audrey had so much work to do that she passed on the invite but promised that she would give them a rain check. The next day she told Kayleigh about the invitation from Jason. Audrey was surprised because he hadn't mentioned anything to her about it. The two had been dating for over three months and Audrey still hadn't met Jason. Every time she would call Kayleigh, Jason would grab the phone and start jokingly asking about the rain check promised.

He was adamant about meeting Kayleigh's friend. After church one Sunday, Audrey finally spent the evening with Kayleigh and Jason. He had grilled some chicken, made a pot of collard greens, macaroni and cheese and rice and gravy. Jason reminded her of how an old grandma would cook, he knew his way around the kitchen. Kayleigh was happy that Audrey finally got a chance to meet her soul mate. Jason was about ten years older than Kayleigh, but she didn't seem to mind the age difference, he was so much fun to be around.

Over the months, Jason and Audrey started to have a big brother, little sister relationship. He started telling Audrey what she should look for in the opposite sex. Jason was super friendly, so friendly that he started to call Audrey to come over for dinner before Kayleigh made it home from work. Out of respect for her friend, she declined because she started to feel like three was a crowd. One weekend, Kayleigh and Audrey was going out and Jason stopped by to make sure the outfits that they were wearing were suitable for his taste. Jason started making comments about Audrey and her little black dress, telling her that the dress was nice, but it was showing too many of her curves. He never commented about the outfit his girlfriend Kayleigh was wearing. Jason told Audrey that she was a great catch, but he wanted to make sure she didn't catch the wrong one.

On the way out the door, Jason straightened the seam on the back of Audrey's dress, near her rear end, telling her that she would be turning heads with that dress. He also mentioned that he loved her beautiful long, flowing hair. Jason shocked them both by saying, "I wish Kayleigh would let her hair grow out so it would hang pretty like yours." Audrey told him not to compare, because Kayleigh was a beautiful diva with her layered bob cut. Kayleigh stated, "Thanks girl, he is always comparing us." It was a wonderful girl's night out together at the jazz club.

Months had passed and occasionally Audrey would stop and eat dinner with Kayleigh and Jason. When Audrey would ask Jason if he had any cute friends, he would answer, "You are out of their league." For a while, Audrey would distance herself from the couple, and Jason would call to check on her, while Kayleigh was still at work. That next year, Jason proposed to Kayleigh. Audrey was so happy for them and couldn't wait to be a part of their wedding. Audrey started noticing whenever Jason and Kayleigh would invite her out with friends, Jason was super protective of anyone that approached her. She felt that he was taking his role as her big brother too serious but was happy that he was always looking out for her. After the two love birds became one, Audrey started spending more time alone reading and writing, something that she loved to do.

She attended some dinner dates with the newlyweds but didn't want to pry in their relationship. Jason always made comments about Audrey and her curves, which started to feel awkward, especially since he was married to Kayleigh. A few years later, the friendship was still going strong when Audrey met a very nice guy that worked in her building. She couldn't wait to introduce him to her friends, visualizing that one day they would all go on a double date.

After three months of dating, they all met for the first time at a mutual friend's wedding. When Audrey introduced Jason and Kayleigh to her new friend Daniel, Jason pulled her to the side and said, "I don't like him." Audrey couldn't believe how judgmental Jason could be, it was like he didn't want to see her in a relationship. Daniel was very sweet; he was excited about meeting Audrey's friends but instead was given the cold shoulder. Kayleigh was friendly but Jason was very nonchalant and was acting very agitated. Audrey went to the restroom and later Jason followed her. As she came out of the restroom, Jason pulled her around the corner and accused Audrey of being naïve and desperate to find a man.

Audrey wanted to cry because she really valued Jason's opinion about her date, but instead he seemed to act out of jealousy. "I'm not desperate, we really like each other, and he is a good guy, if you would just get to know him," Audrey said. Jason started telling some of the groomsmen about Audrey's date Daniel, asking them to express their thoughts. He was disappointed when they told him that they thought he was overreacting about the situation, and Daniel seemed to be a cool guy. Later that week, Jason and Kayleigh invited Audrey over for a fish fry, something she couldn't resist.

She was ready to discuss with Jason what went wrong at the wedding with her date. Jason was very vocal about telling Audrey how her date was an undercover player, and he loved her so much that he didn't dare want to see her get hurt. Jason mentioned that Daniel probably was only interested in getting her in the bed, nothing serious. Audrey and Jason got into a heated argument, so much, that Kayleigh had to be the mediator. Audrey left teary-eyed because that wasn't how she envisioned the conversation to go. She loved Jason and Kayleigh, but Jason couldn't stand to see her with a boyfriend, it was like he enjoyed seeing her single and depend on them to have a good time. Months had passed and Audrey decided to distance herself from her friends to let everything cool down. She finally called Kayleigh, who seemed happy about the progression of her relationship. She asked to speak with Jason, but he was too busy to talk.

Daniel stopped by to visit Audrey and told her that the reason Jason wouldn't communicate with him at the wedding, was because Jason is in love with her. Daniel told her that Jason enjoys preparing meals so he can get to flirt with his wife's best friend, Audrey. Daniel also mentioned, "I see the way he watches your every move. He wants his cake and eat it too." Audrey couldn't believe what Daniel was saying, and denied Jason's feelings for her, explaining that they had a brother-sister type relationship. After reminiscing on the flirtatious comments Jason had made to her in the past and his actions, she realized that Daniel was right, Jason wanted her and her best friend Kayleigh.

Daniel and Audrey's relationship was going strong, they had only been dating for one year when Daniel started discussing finding his virtuous woman, a wife. He was ready to make things official and start a new life with the one he loved…. Audrey! On their way to a weekend getaway on a secluded beach, Daniel proposed to Audrey. She said "Yes!" It was such a beautiful proposal and Audrey was the happiest girl alive! She waited until she got back to Philly to share the exciting news with Kayleigh and Jason, but to her surprise, she couldn't reach them, their phone numbers had been changed. She called and called, even went by their apartment, and later found out from a neighbor that they had moved. Audrey was devastated because she and Kayleigh had been friends for over five years. When love comes knocking, will she answer?

Kayleigh and Audrey started out as great friends, but it got very complicated when Kayleigh started dating Jason, but as Daniel clearly pointed out, Jason had some deep feelings for Audrey. Daniel was a great guy to Audrey, and although he didn't have the best track record when it came to relationships, he was ready to start something new with Audrey. Jason didn't want Audrey to find her own love because he didn't want anyone else to come between the three of them. He looked forward to the occasional visits from Audrey. His flirtatious ways were very noticeable to his wife Kayleigh, and deep down she knew her husband Jason had a thing for her friend Audrey.

It is sad that Kayleigh and Audrey couldn't openly discuss what was going on, because their friendship was strong before Jason or Daniel came into the picture. Audrey was truly happy when Kayleigh found her true love but because of the infatuation that Jason had for Audrey, Kayleigh couldn't wholeheartedly be there for her friend. Kayleigh didn't want the situation to become worse so to keep her marriage together she had to distance herself.

Sadly, when Kayleigh and Jason became husband and wife, the couple decided to go their separate ways, and no longer be friends with Audrey and Daniel because they felt it would be better for everyone. It is sad, but sometimes friendships come and go. Your true friends want the very best for you and want to see you happy. Choose your friends wisely and if they don't respect the decisions you make for your life and the companion you decide to be with, unless they have good reason, you may have to part ways. Daniel and Audrey decided to let their love shine bright. They have been happily married for 16 years with three beautiful children.

Chapter 3

Never Say Never

Saying things unpleasing like, I wouldn't ever date a fat man, a man that isn't making six figures, a man that doesn't own his own home, a man that has a child, been married before, a short man, or a man that drives an old car. Keep living because it is always important to never say you will never do something. God has a plan for all of our lives. Maybe that short man will treat you like a queen, and you will be blessed to live in peace and happiness. You may be looking for a husband or wife that will be your forever eye candy.

No matter the flavor you like, everyone has problems. Everyone has a story, and you don't know what obstacles he or she had to face in life. He may be driving an old car to work to save on gas or save for something better. He just may have something nicer parked at home. Don't be so critical. Life can bring about situational changes to anyone. Your life is not perfect, so before you start judging, learn to be open to get to know a person for who they are, not for what they have. People change every day. You may be skinny now, but if you are blessed with children one day, you will have to deal with body changes. What if your husband rejects your post baby body because you have changed? There are some men that feel having a voluptuous body is attractive. Always remember that your life should not be compared to no one else's. Check your standards, because whether they are too high or low, you must be able to accept people for what they are and what they are not.

A little girl dreams of having a happily ever after life. She visualizes a wedding with all the frills and lace imaginable. Keep dreaming because it may come true. A marriage is not a wedding, it is a lifelong commitment between two imperfect people that is willing to work together for a common goal. It is having unconditional love and forgiveness between the good and bad times. It is to know that having it all, doesn't always mean having it all at once.

You are very attractive but understand that everyone that comes along is not marriage material. They may be someone to hang out with to keep you occupied until you meet the right one. If you are single, it is ok to have a friend, a dinner partner, or a movie buddy, and friendship etiquette is a must.

If he or she shows you a good time, learn to keep it mutual so you don't feel that you must put out. It is ok for the woman to take care of the bill, especially if she was the one to extend the invite. Always remember that independence goes a long way. At least offer to pay your portion, and maybe if he is a true gentleman, he will immediately refuse your request and pick up the tab. Guys should not expect any sexual activity because they have wined and dined you for the evening. If she orders the most expensive item on the menu, it doesn't give you the right to expect to be rolling around in the sack. If there is a next time, you pick a nice restaurant but less pricey. Make sure he or she knows that you are just friends. Communicate and make it plain so that there won't be any expectations at the close of the night.

Makena is a high-powered criminal defense attorney, and she isn't afraid to work hard, but also know how to enjoy the fruits of her labor. There were several good guys that crossed Makena's path within her life, but she was so busy finding their wrong, that she failed to see some of their right. Makena has always viewed herself as top notch and very judgmental when approached by anyone.

She's a know-it-all and seems to get a thrill from demeaning others. Her and her girlfriend decided to relive the movie, "How Stella Got Her Groove Back," and took a trip to Jamaica. Makena is celebrating her 40th birthday and ready to let loose and celebrate life. As she enters the plane, everyone is greeted by the pilot that looked very familiar. Makena arrived at her destination, Jamaica, and her girlfriend has set up a beautiful birthday celebration for her through the concierge at the hotel. It was quite the surprise. Makena had the best time in Jamaica. It was truly a well-deserved getaway with her girlfriend, but she couldn't seem to stop thinking about the airplane pilot.

Makena felt that she has met the pilot before and wishes she could have gotten his name. She meets other guys on the island, and have a great time, but her mind continues to wonder. Makena lands back home and as she is getting off the plane, she sees that same pilot and immediately ask his name. She is baffled to find out that he went to high school with her. Efraim had a crush on Makena in school, but because he was a nerd, not popular, and didn't fit her standards of what a dream guy should look like, she didn't give him a chance. He approached her only once while in high school, but because he heard how she would demean guys, he never asked her out on a date. Makena was very popular and didn't hesitate in letting guys know how she felt about them, good or bad. Her attitude was horrible, and she had judgmental ways, which pushed a lot of them away.

Fast forward, it is now 20 years later, and Makena has been complaining that there are no more good men in the world. She has been begging God for years to send her a good man, but if the package is not what she expected on the outside, she rejects them. Efraim is a good man with morals and values and always has been gentle-hearted. He has gotten his master's degree, graduated from pilot school, and received his pilot license. He has been flying commercial airplanes for 10 years, a widow, and a single dad raising his three-year-old daughter Simone. Everyone knows that Makena doesn't date anyone that has a child because of prior issues she has had with men and children.

Twenty years later, it is evident that there are some sparks between the two of them. Makena goes on a date, and the two just can't seem to get enough of each other. Months later, Makena meets his daughter Simone for the first time, and instantly falls in love with her. Simone's Mom passed away when she was only a year old. Makena has a bond with Efraim and Simone and can't see herself without the two of them. Efraim adores Makena and is thinking about asking for her hand in marriage. After about 6 months of dating, his three-year-old daughter Simone starts to call Makena, Mommy. When love comes knocking, will she answer?

Life can be full of surprises. God can bless us when we least expect it. We all may have expectations of what our Mr. Right will look like but learn to trust God's plan for our lives. Makena realized that sometimes we must humble ourselves to receive the blessings from God. She seemed to be willing and ready to start a new life with Efraim and his daughter Simone. God knows all and sees all. The nerds of yesterday may just be the CEOs and Presidents of tomorrow. Learn to treat others how you would like to be treated. Although you are wiser than you were in your past, always remember when you demean an individual, you make them feel worthless, doubtful, insecure and creates the attitude that no one cares. This is very damaging to one's self-esteem and self-confidence, and it may cause them to display anger and hostility.

In a relationship, you must allow people to be unique in their own way. Don't be a know-it-all, be teachable because you are not always right. Treat people kind, there is enough criticism in the world. If you meet a guy and he isn't what you expected him to be, try to get to know him first. If he is not what you like, just move on, but don't tear down an entire group because of the hurt you went through with someone else. When God is in control, all things work out for our good. Trust the process and believe that he has all power in his hands.

Chapter 4

I'm Not Your Mama

Alton is ready to settle down and be a one-woman man. His future wife must be able to cook and clean like his Mama. Be a nurturer like his Mama, respect and obey like his Mama does his Daddy, and give him sexual pleasures anytime he asks for it. She must be stacked, thirty-six, twenty-four, thirty-six, cute face and slim waist with a big behind. Alton is very vocal about what he wants in a wife, and there are no compromises. He is very educated, making a six-figure salary and does not want his future wife working outside the home. He is very domineering and expresses what he wants in life to anyone he meets.

Savannah is introduced to him by her friend Marie, who tells her about him because she is motivated by his rich, flashy lifestyle. Marie's husband, Juan, is one of Alton's friends who also flaunts his money, but what Marie doesn't tell Savannah is that although her husband buys her whatever she wants, she is constantly dealing with physical abuse. Savannah has always been an independent woman, making her own money, not having to look for any handouts, but she is tired of being alone. She wants to settle down and have children but can't seem to find anyone. She goes out on several dates with Alton, and he is watching her body like it is meat on the entrée. She's flattered but feels like he is too caught up in her looks instead of what is inside her heart. Alton constantly talks about his career and when she tries to discuss hers, he seems uninterested.

Many months he is showering her with just because gifts, weekend getaways, and shopping sprees. He tells her about his expectations for his future wife and reiterates again that she won't be working outside of the home, not even considering what his future wife wants to do. Alton loves children and wants many, but he is adamant that his wife won't lose her curves and will stay fit. Savannah has seen some signs of extreme anger when the waiter mistakenly got Alton's order mixed up with another customer. Alton wants to get married and live happily ever after with Savannah. When love comes knocking, will she answer?

There are red flags flashing everywhere. Don't be naïve and desperate. You have a great life and being alone doesn't necessarily mean that you are lonely. This guy is comparing you to his Mama, which is a definite "No, no!" When you are married there should be mutual respect. You should love and respect your husband, just like he should love and respect his wife. You must learn to speak up for your beliefs, but it is obvious that there won't be any compromising in this relationship, because he seems to be caught up in his own selfish ways, that he won't take the time to understand your needs and desires.

You see signs of anger issues while dating, adios amigos! It will probably get worse before it gets better. Alton taking out his anger on the waiter, next time he will be taking it out on you. He is looking for a wife to stay "bare foot and pregnant," as the saying goes. You won't have any goals and aspirations of your own. Your job will be to cook, clean, take care of the children and give him pleasure. If your girlfriend Marie was a true friend, she would be open about the abuse that she has to deal with from her husband, Juan. This may save you from a lifetime of hurt, but she is too focused on spending money, that she is willing to take the abuse from him. Please don't gain weight after the babies are born because you may just get tossed away. He should want you to have a successful career and build a life together with you. You deserve to be treated with kindness and respect. Love yourself so much that you would rather live alone in happiness, instead of living wealthy in misery. Always choose love and appreciation, never domination.

Jackson William Alexander III has a great career, a beautiful condo in downtown Houston and a nice set of wheels to get him around the city. He is the only child and a true Mama's boy. Jackson is a Houston City Councilman, named after his father and his grandfather. Houston, also known as H-town is the fourth largest city in the United States. It is home to the national champions Houston Astros and Houston Rockets; other sports teams are the Houston Texans (formerly Houston Oilers) and the Houston Dynamo. It is closely linked to Space Center Houston, NASA's astronaut, and flight control complex.

Houston has a wonderful Theater District, renowned Grand Opera, host several festivals throughout the year and many city attractions. It is the hub in oil and gas and has the largest medical center in the world. There are also more than 145 different languages spoken in Houston. Houstonians love the stable job market, affordable neighborhoods, and the diverse economy. Residents find it hard to be on a diet in Houston because there are thousands of restaurants in the Houston area with culinary choices that represent more than 70 countries and American regions.

There are many favorite black-owned restaurants, such as, Lucille's, Phil & Derek's, The Breakfast Klub, The Stuffed Potato Factory, The Turkey Leg Hut, Cool Runnings Jamaican Grill, Houston This Is It Soul Food, Alfreda's Soul Food, Krab Kingz, Cupcake Kitchen Houston, Sugar's Cajun Cuisine & Bar, Mikki's Soul Food, and Esther's Cajun Café Soul Food. Houstonians truly enjoy their dining out experience, many eating out more than six times per week.

Jackson is well known in the city. He loves his mom Gladys unconditionally but can't seem to get her to like anyone he dates. His political career has been in many media outlets, representing Houston, the city that he loves so dearly. His personal life is suffering, because every girlfriend he had, his mom ran them away, always finding something wrong with them. Some of these women were truly in love with him, but as soon as they met his Mama, everything went downhill. Jackson's dad passed away and he doesn't mind his Mama dating again, but she feels like that would be cheating on his dad, who has been deceased for over a decade.

Gladys, Jackson's mom is very active in the church, and several of the men find her attractive, but she doesn't give them the time of day. She continues to explain that her new love is King Jesus. Jackson doesn't want to hurt his Mama, because when no one else was there, she was always in his corner supporting his dreams. Jackson was the bread winner and the man of the house after his dad passed. He loves his mom but when he wakes up in the morning, his mom calls to check to see what he ate for breakfast, also checking to make sure he is at work on time.

Every day she is checking on his plans for the day. Jackson doesn't know how to tell her to back off without hurting her feelings. There is a new love in Jackson's life, and he has been secretly dating Henley for nine months, without his Mama's knowledge. He has been avoiding some of his Mama's calls and feels guilty. Jackson met Henley's parents and almost her entire family when she recently asked to meet his mom. Henley, who is 25, is the oldest of three children, comes from a very close family and lives in a downtown studio apartment. She is a registered nurse and is very independent. Jackson is in love with her and doesn't want anything to mess up the relationship. He is really thinking about popping the big question to her. He wants to talk with his Mama, but she has always been so vocal in his relationships, which is partly his fault.

Gladys has always had issues with Jackson's past dates because she feels like no one is good enough for her son. She always thought his dates were using him for his money. Sometimes he feels that his Mama fears that his new love will take her place, because he always pampers her with gifts and money. Without having a conversation with his Mama, Jackson finally gets the nerve to introduce Henley to her and she immediately gives her the cold shoulder. Henley is a beautiful person inside and out, and Jackson would like his Mama to like her, but as usual she is trying to find fault in her. His Mom sees that he won't let her win, and that Henley may be the one, so she starts to dig up dirt on Henley and her family. She finds out through a mutual friend that Henley's Mom cheated on her dad years ago and tells Jackson that the women of that family are not to be trusted.

Gladys secretly watches Henley's morning routine and asked a co-worker to go to the local kolache and donut shop to flirt with her. Henley doesn't fall for the trick and quickly brushes off his mom's co-workers' flirtatious gestures. Gladys always had a problem with his girlfriends, either his women friends were too tall, short, fat, skinny, suspicious that they wanted his money, they have a child or just come from the wrong family. Jackson has secretly purchased an engagement ring to give to Henley on her birthday. Henley respects his Mama, but feels she is not letting Jackson be a man and make his own choices for his life. Henley and Mama Gladys doesn't see eye to eye. When love comes knocking, will she answer?

Jackson must stand up to his Mama because she may never like anyone, he introduces her to. Your Mama has your best interest, but it seems that she doesn't have a life of her own, therefore she is always trying to control yours. You will be old and lonely if you continue to allow your Mama to dictate who you can date. You must speak with your mom in a loving and respectful way so that she will understand that you are a grown man, old enough to make your own decisions, especially when it comes to women. You have allowed her to have a say so in your relationships for way too long, and now it is hard for her to back away. Let her know that she has raised you to have a good judgment of character, but she must take a back seat and allow you to be the driver of your own relationships.

There is no perfect person or family. This is your life and whether you make mistakes, it will be a learning experience. She cannot shelter you from the hurts of life, what won't break you, will make you stronger. You have a great woman in your life, you love her, and she loves you. You cannot let your Mama come in between something that may manifest into a forever relationship. You should assure her that you will continue to love her and be there for her, because she will always be your Mama. You don't have to choose between your Mama and your girlfriend, each one has an important place in your heart. Maybe one day you can invite them both on a date to get to know each other better. You must require respect, because you have allowed your Mama to take control for so long, it may take some adjustments on her part.

Encourage your mom to go out with friends and consider dating. If she had a social life, it would take some of the attention from you and yours. Be patient and give her the time that she needs. Be the man God has created you to be. You don't have to be rude or disrespectful to let your Mama know where you stand. Explain to your girlfriend the relationship you have with your mom. You are close to your mom and every woman should appreciate that, because it will be a way you show her how you will hopefully love and respect her.

Lastly, Mama cannot pop up anytime at your condo anymore. She must call you first, because remember you are a grown man. Have limits on the just because gifts and money given to your mom, because whenever you get married, you don't want this to cause confusion in your marriage. Finances can add stress to the relationship. You may want to start weaning her off from getting money and gifts so often. Your Mom and girlfriend are your greatest treasures. They both have something in common, they love you dearly. Have effective communication, because you never want to be in a situation where you feel you must choose between the two of them. There is no competition, you must be the man, and set boundaries.

Chapter 5

Honesty Is the Best Policy

Being in love is the best feeling in the world, but the love shared should be between two people. Aviana goes on a blind date that her best friend Keegan sets up for her. She is very appreciative that her best friend wants her to be happy and find true love. Aviana's date Diego is a gentleman, very good looking, and has a great career. He is perfect in every way but seems to love talking about his friendship he has with Keegan. They were friends many years ago, but they lost contact and the friendship dwindled away. Aviana doesn't know the specific details of their friendship but has become suspicious because Keegan seems to always pop up in the conversations. Aviana and Diego are getting closer and decides to meet each other's families. Keegan has so many friends and later Aviana finds out that Diego is keeping open communication with her.

While at the restaurant with Diego, Aviana noticed Keegan is there with her boyfriend. After dinner, they go to the movies and her best friend Keegan pops up there too. The next day, Aviana calls Diego to let him know what great time she had on the date, and is interrupted by an incoming call from Keegan, who is venting to Diego about her boyfriend. This is really starting to get under Aviana's skin, but Keegan is her best friend, and because of her, she has met this wonderful man, Diego. The situation is annoying and stresses Aviana to her limits because it is affecting her sleep, work, even the relationship with her and Diego. When Aviana asked Diego about his friendship with Keegan, he mentioned that they are only friends. It has been four months and Aviana is falling in love with Diego, and he seems to be feeling the same way towards her. She feels like although her best friend Keegan has a special someone, she still uses her boyfriend Diego as her go to person.

Aviana finally gets up the courage to tell Keegan how she feels about the friendship that she has with her boyfriend. Keegan immediately gets defensive, telling her that if it wasn't for her, she wouldn't have met Diego. Aviana is upset because at the peak of the argument, Keegan shared with her that they weren't just friends, they were lovers. Aviana was livid! When she asked Diego, he finally admitted that they were intimate, but only once. Aviana becomes distant from Keegan and Diego for not telling her the whole truth. Diego tries to explain to Aviana that the chapter with Keegan is closed and he wants her and only her, even mentioning marriage. Aviana is totally confused. When love comes knocking, will she answer?

Honesty is the best policy and Aviana's friends weren't honest and open with her. Aviana should have asked more questions at the beginning when her best friend introduced her to Diego. Keegan is your best friend, and it should have been a conversation between the two of you, to make sure that you were comfortable dating your best friend's ex-lover. Keegan wasn't being 100% truthful, which could damage your friendship. Your boyfriend Diego is not in the clear because he may have an attraction with the both of you. Keegan was his ex-lover and there may still be lingering feelings. Also, do you really believe that they were only intimate once?

Parting ways is an option because you will always be suspicious of their relationship, and if you decide to become an official couple, will he run back to Keegan if the two of you have a disagreement? When you meet someone, and you feel it may turn into a potential relationship, ask as many questions as you can think of. If they have a problem with answering the questions, or seem to shy away, it may be a reason for you to run for the hills.

Love is for better or worse. I read a poem once by an anonymous author that read, "May you have enough happiness to keep you sweet, enough trials to keep you strong, enough sorrow to keep you human, enough hope to keep you happy, enough failure to keep you humble, enough success to keep you eager, enough friends to give you comfort, enough faith and courage in yourself to banish depression, enough wealth to meet your needs, enough determination to make each day better than yesterday."

When you say, "I Do," you are committing to sticking through all the trials and tribulations that you may endure during your walk of life together. Make sure your commitment is to the person that you love and trust. Marriage is no joke, and it is better to know what you are getting yourself into before you commit to a lifetime of hurt and pain. Ask questions.

Chicago is a beautiful city, with delicious cuisines, beautiful downtown architecture, music, sports, festivals, art and history museums and home of former President Barack and Michelle Obama. It is a melting pot of different cultures and lifestyles. Jiao Ling is the top real estate agent in the area. She has sold residential and commercial properties from the Lincoln Park area to the South side of Chicago.

Life is great for Jiao because she has worked very hard to get to where she is today. She moved to the United States 10 years ago with her parents and siblings who spoke very little English. Jiao attended college and stayed in the library, educating herself to understand the language of the land. Jiao also taught her parents to speak English, and they now own several businesses in the city. Her parents meant the world to her, and Jiao valued her parent's opinion on everything. She was the second oldest of four children and was highly respected within the family.

Jiao was very successful and years later started her own real estate company. Her business was very well known throughout the mid-west. Jiao was asked to help a client's son find property near Uptown. He was a very nice Vietnamese banker named Hien Khan that had just moved to Chicago. Jiao was a true professional and never mixed business with pleasure, but there was something different about Hien, he was a true gentleman. Looking at a lot of properties worked up an appetite and they both decided to enjoy happy hour at a Mediterranean restaurant. They found out that they liked a lot of the same things, it was unbelievable how they connected so quickly.

Jiao went home and couldn't get Hien out of her mind, but she needed to stay focused. A few days had passed, and Hien called her to see more properties, when surprisingly, he shared that he felt an attraction for her. He told her that he had a connection with her that he had never experienced with anyone. Jiao was shocked, but felt the exact same way, but was afraid to love again. She had been deeply hurt by her ex-boyfriend and never wanted to date again.

Hien was true to his name which meant kind, nice and gentle in Vietnamese. Jiao was Chinese and didn't know how her family would accept her dating a guy from Vietnam. Jiao's parents weren't very fond of the Vietnamese culture because they had several negative business encounters, and they never wanted to mix families. Jiao always respected her parent's opinions but wanted to make her own decisions when it came to matters of the heart.

Jiao believed in treating all people with kindness and respect, often enjoying her girlfriends who were from different backgrounds. Hien was a high-powered banker, who was the youngest to have a seat on the board of directors with a popular bank in Illinois. Jiao's parents had expanded their businesses and needed a loan. They met with a loan officer and because additional information was needed, they had to have their paperwork reviewed.

Jiao decided to tell them about her friend Hien, and immediately they told her that they disapproved of the relationship, explaining to her that they wanted her to meet someone of her own kind. Her parents told her that they only wanted to have Chinese grandchildren. They asked Jiao to promise never to see him again. She agreed but knew she couldn't control the feelings she had for Hien. She decided they would continue to see each other but would just keep things quiet.

Hien understood her parent's point of view because his parents were the same way with the Chinese culture. Hien was truly falling in love with Jiao. He told her not to worry because things would eventually work itself out. He had strong feelings for her and didn't want to lose her because of their family's traditional ways of thinking. They both felt their parents needed to be a little bit more modernized.

Jiao's parents had to meet with a banker to get a previous loan increased and extended. She met her parents at the bank to help them communicate, because they weren't pros of the English language yet. Jiao knew Hien was a banker but didn't realize exactly what he did or what branch he worked for. When they arrived at the bank and entered the office of the banker, you wouldn't believe who had to approve their loan? Yes, it was Hien! He was in total shock because this is his first time ever meeting her parents. When love comes knocking, will Jiao and Hien answer?

Your parents want the best for you, but sometimes they must realize what may have worked for them, may not work for you. Parents must allow their children to live their own lives. Judging a culture as a whole because of a bad experience is a way you are showing your ignorance and insecurities. You are preventing yourself from seeing the good character traits and love that lies beyond a person's background and culture. It seems to be the people that know you the least are the ones to judge you the most. You must accept people for who they are, not from where they come from.

Never look down on anyone because you are still living. Like Jiao's parents, that person that you dislike may be the one you have to lean on for help. Sometimes you dislike someone based on someone else's beliefs, and you haven't gotten a chance to get to know them for yourself. A lot of people stereotype other cultures, but everybody is different. There is a story behind every person, and a reason why they act the way they do. Always think about that the next time you want to judge. Maybe you don't understand their culture, educate yourself and learn to embrace diversity.

As a baby you are not born with hate in your heart, this is something that is taught. If you dislike a race because of the color of someone's skin, ask yourself why? Maybe it is a generational curse from your parent's teachings. This crazy way of thinking is triggering down to you. When will you stop the curse? There is good and evil in all cultures, don't be judgmental.

What if you don't like a particular race and you are on your death bed, and the very race you despise, is the one to give you an organ to save your life, will you refuse to live? You judge because you haven't walked in that person's shoes. You must learn to be open-minded and allow your children to find love their own way. Life can be difficult, and they may face some challenges, but it is part of growth. God is the only one who can judge. Love conquers all.

Trisha and her boyfriend Tobias are from Washington D.C. and have been dating for four years. There is no doubt in her mind that he will be her forever companion. He has shown her that she is his soul mate, and his searching days are behind him. Trisha loves his family, and he loves hers. The two of them have gone ring shopping a few times, but Trisha is now waiting patiently for that special moment. Tobias works in construction and is a fitness guru, often taking showers on the job site, and sometimes working out with his co-workers after work. The construction company he works for is very well known in the city, building the city's tallest skyscrapers and million-dollar homes. Tobias has been in construction since working with his dad as a little boy, in hopes of one day owning his very own company. He and his boss are very close, but Trisha feels that his boss has some unhidden motives, but she doesn't have any proof.

Every time Trisha surprises her boyfriend for lunch, she feels there is a sense of dislike towards her from his boss. Trisha mentioned it to Tobias, but he says it is all in her head. His boss appears to be a workaholic, loves hanging out with his crew, and doesn't seem to have a life of his own. One day Trisha decides to play private investigator and creates an anonymous social media page to snoop on his boss. His profile picture is him and another grown man locked arm to arm. Trisha doesn't know if this is his partner or a family member. There are a few women on his page, but mainly guys who are buffed, just like her boyfriend Tobias.

She tries to focus on her own career as a director of event planning for a catering and hospitality company, but it is very hard because her intuition is speaking loud and clear. Trisha is excited because she gets to show off her skills, hosting an Annual Pride Gala for the LGBT community. Although she has her own beliefs, this opportunity will boost her career to another level.

This event is so huge that it takes a lot of her time and attention from her boyfriend. It was an awesome night! Trisha grazes the crowd and low and behold, Tobias's boss is sitting in the audience. He is a businessman, so she doesn't know if he is representing his company, representing his lifestyle or both. Many months later, Trisha notices her boyfriend has been very distant. She didn't realize Tobias was planning to swift her away on a romantic getaway to the Cayman Islands to propose to her. He had shared the news of making Trisha his wife to his boss and co-workers, and everyone seemed excited. Tobias's dream was finally coming true when his boss approached him about an opportunity to show his leadership skills. His boss announced that Tobias would be the Project Manager on a multi-million-dollar estate to be built in the suburbs of Washington, D.C. Tobias was thrilled!

His boss gave him the blueprint of the community and scheduled meetings with the contractors, the same day they were supposed to go on their romantic getaway. His boss also mentioned that he had networked with other contractors about starting a subsidiary of their company, which will give Tobias the opportunity to have his own company, and investors were anxiously waiting. This was a dream come true for Tobias! He was in his early 30's and had waited since he was a teenager for this opportunity. Tobias always knew that his hard work would pay off.

Sadly, he was heartbroken that he had to cancel the trip to the Cayman Islands, later telling Trisha about his plans. She was upset about this and didn't speak to Tobias for days. Trisha had been so busy she had forgotten to mention to him that his boss attended the Annual Pride LGBT event. That event brought in over a quarter of a million dollars, which would be an increase for her and her employees.

43

At the event Trisha left survey cards on the table, and she was so happy that they were all positive, giving her business a rating of five stars for exceptional service, except for one that stated that the hosting was poor, and the food lacked seasoning. Trisha knew that Tobias's boss made the negative comment because she knew his handwriting. Every time Tobias planned to enjoy some quality time with Trisha, it was interrupted by something work related.

Trisha was so ready to say, "I Do," and after four years, she didn't care if the proposal was at a shopping mall. One day when Tobias came over, he told Trisha that he caught his boss staring at him from a distance in a lustful way. Trisha knew her intuition didn't lead her wrong, but Tobias still didn't let it affect him from working long hours and accepting construction projects, which has been putting a strain on their relationship. When love comes knocking, will she answer?

Trisha and Tobias seem to have a very promising relationship. Their love is very evident for each other, they both seem to want the same things, but they have very busy work schedules. They must decide to make their relationship a priority and maybe if they can't go on a romantic getaway to an island, they can find somewhere just as special in the city. When you find true love, you must be careful who you share your good news with, because others may be jealous. Although Tobias's boss may have a slight crush on him, as an employer he cannot cross that line, but it is left up to Tobias to set the boundaries.

Hopefully, it won't jeopardize his networking opportunities. Whether his boss is infatuated with him or not, he should continue to acknowledge his efforts and promote him accordingly. Tobias seems to be focused so much on accomplishing his career goals that he is prolonging his relationship goals. After four years of dating, it may be time to put a ring on it! There are a lot of distractions, and your partner may feel like she is number two on your list of priorities. Pray and seek counseling. Let's hope Tobias makes a conscious effort to propose to Trisha before it is too late.

44

Chapter 6

Your Past Makes a Present Appearance

Manuel sees a nice woman every morning on his way to work who he can't seem to get out of his mind. He watches her on the subway looking so beautiful wearing a two-piece suit and carrying her briefcase. He assumes she has a good job working in corporate America. Manuel works behind the scenes, a journalist at a local news firm and would like to become acquainted with this young lady. She is always reading, and he doesn't want to bother her, but he is unsure how many chances he will have to connect with her. When she reaches her stop, Manuel runs up to her and says, "Good Morning my name is Manuel." She replies with a smile and continues to walk to work.

Manuel tries to start a conversation, but it is obvious that she is in a hurry. He tells her that he has been noticing her on the subway and wanted to meet her. He invites her to get breakfast one morning or meet her at the local café for dinner. Surprisingly, she says that would be nice, and introduces herself, "Hello, my name is Reign." Manuel is so happy to exchange phone numbers. That next day, Manuel meets her for dinner and finds out that she is a high school counselor and founder of a non-profit organization for teen girls. Manuel feels that he has struck the jackpot because a lot of women he had met over the years didn't have promising careers, and seemed to look at him for a paycheck, not being independent in having their own money. Manuel is so happy that he and Reign have a lot in common.

For months Manuel feels so connected to Reign and starts to have some deep feelings for her. Her family is originally from El Salvador and Manuel is from Puerto Rico. The two of them have plans to one day meet each other's families. Manuel noticed that her name Reign, is very different from your typical El Salvadorian name, but she explained how she changed it when she moved to the United States.

Reign mentioned that she was thinking about changing it again because it was a product of her past. When Manuel wanted to ask her what she was talking about, she quickly changed the subject. Months later he had some research to do at work. The story seemed quite interesting and intense, and he couldn't wait to get on this project. Manuel and Reign were becoming an official couple. His family was coming to Miami to visit, and he couldn't wait for them to meet her. One Saturday, Manuel took Reign to a local restaurant, when this guy passed by and said, "Hey I know you." "Make it rain Reign!" He passed by laughing and chanting it multiple times. Reign had an ashamed look on her face. When Manuel asked her about the comment, she said, "Oh that guy was just being goofy."

As Manuel goes back to work the next day, he constantly thinks of the comment made by the guy and the look on his girlfriend's face. He felt like she had been hiding something. The next day, Manuel's boss gives him a picture to include in his project, he sees that it is about a former exotic dancer, and it is his girlfriend Reign! Manuel can't breathe, he starts to feel sick. The article was about a former exotic dancer who changed her life and became a high school counselor to help teenage girls get off the street and learn to use their minds instead of their bodies to be an asset to society. Manuel doesn't know whether to call her, change his number, or cry. He has finally met someone that he felt a strong connection with and was truly falling in love with. When love comes knocking, will he answer?

Communication, communication, and more communication. Everyone has a past and a story to tell and you surely want to hear hers. Ask Reign about the article you read and listen closely and carefully without judgement. Reign had been very quiet about her past and talking about her family. Manuel invites her over to his apartment and finally gets up the nerve to tell her about the news article. She immediately starts to cry because she assumes it will change the direction of the relationship. Reign opens up about her past telling him when she moved to the United States, at the young age of 16 her parents were on drugs, and not fit to care for the family. She decided to drop out of school, to make some quick money to care for her younger siblings, because she was the oldest.

At the age of 16, she started dancing at an underground teen club until she was 22. Although she made some good money, and they didn't go lacking for anything, she hated herself and had low self-esteem for becoming a stripper. Reign went on to say, she is still dealing with demons from her past, and it is hard for her to forgive herself and move forward.

Her parents finally got off drugs and were able to care for her and her siblings. She went back to school and got her GED and decided to enroll in community college. Four years later, she graduated from college, got her counselor's certification, and founded a non-profit organization to help other girls in similar situations. The guy at the restaurant was one of her past customers at the strip club. She opens up about hating that type of lifestyle, but didn't know what else to do, because she had to help raise her 5 siblings. She explained to Manuel that her and her dad has a very distant relationship. He cannot forgive himself for putting his own daughter in a situation to use her body for money.

Manuel was at a loss for words, he came to the realization that everyone has a past, and you cannot judge people for their mistakes. He forgave Reign because that was who she was, but he had fallen in love with the woman she had become. He was so happy to introduce her to his family. He wrote the article and was not ashamed to admit to his co-workers that it was his best piece of work, because it was very close to his heart. Manuel suggested that they all go to counseling, and he would be right by her and her family's side. He stayed fair-minded and prayed that God could help her forgive the old Reign and celebrate the new person that God had made her to be. Manuel was so proud of how Reign was a blessing to others; her trials of life became a true testimony.

It is so important to forgive yourself for the mistakes you've made in life. If you don't, it can make you feel like a hostage in your own body, and hinder the blessings that God has for you. Life is about learning and gaining wisdom, we don't always make the right decisions, but God allows us to repent of our sins and try again. Live without regrets and forgive yourself and others.

Chapter 7

Children Need Love Too

Chioma met a guy named Ifechi at a restaurant in Lagos, Nigeria, where they are both from. They have been dating for five months. He is very loving, thoughtful, and seemed to have it all together. Ifechi is divorced and has a six-year-old daughter named Lebechi, and he refuses to spend any time with her because of his strong dislike for his daughter's mother. He and his ex-wife divorced when his daughter was only two. The couple decided not to have a court ordered visitation years ago. They made a verbal agreement of what they wanted, and he only pays child support.

Chioma had very strong feelings about this set up because she grew up without having a relationship with her dad. Lagos has so much to offer. When she was younger, she often wondered how it would be to go to a Daddy daughter's dance, visits to historic museums, shop at the open air markets, have someone to teach you how to ride a bike, enjoy reading together, canoe through the mangroves to get a taste of Nigerian nature, enjoy a picnic at the park, ride a Keke, or taxi, soak in the sun at the beach or just spend quality time together with her Dad.

Chioma enjoyed fun times with her mom, but it is nothing like having a relationship with both parents. Ifechi had been talking about settling down with Chioma, but often he seemed sad when he saw posts of his baby girl Lebechi on social media. Him and his ex-wife were very stubborn and hadn't made their daughter's need a priority. Chioma loved Ifechi but felt like she was re-living the hurt of her own Dad being absent in her life.

Chioma has constantly shared her feelings with Ifechi about the situation with her and her dad growing up. When she wanted to communicate about them gaining a relationship with his six-year-old daughter, Ifechi completely changed the subject. Chioma loves everything about this man, except his contentment of just providing for his daughter financially. He doesn't seem to care about spending quality time with her. After five months of dating, Ifechi proposes and confesses his eternal love to Chioma. When love comes knocking, will she answer?

Chioma is doing right by speaking up at the beginning about the relationship and sharing stories of the missing piece of the puzzle called her dad. It takes time to build a relationship with a loved one, but it is never too late. His life is relatable to hers, because her dad wasn't there, and letting him know the void she felt in her own life, as a child into adulthood, would probably help him to better understand the importance of building a relationship with his daughter. Men and women can be very stubborn individuals, but sometimes you may need a woman-to-woman intervention.

Several women face similar situations, but you must realize that you didn't have any history with neither of them. Your stance should be neutral. You will have a commitment with Ifechi, so you will be involved, and as the wife and stepmom, your voice should be heard. Since Ifechi won't be the bigger person, maybe you should woman up, say a prayer and look out for the best interest of your soon to be stepdaughter, Lebechi. There may have been some underlined situations that occurred in the marriage that you may not be aware of, but it is still no excuse to divorce a child.

Schedule a time that you and Ifechi's ex can have a sit-down talk. Your conversation should be warm, loving, and respectful. This won't be an easy task, but you should focus on making the child a priority and put all other feelings aside. When all the bickering has subsided, the child will still have to suffer from not having the love from both parents. Seek love and understanding, because divorce is already hard, especially if a child is involved. Have effective communication with each other, because sometimes arguments occur because of lack of understanding. Mean what you say and say what you mean. If you commit to picking the child up at a certain time, stick to it! This is already very hard to endure, but you are leaving the other parent to make excuses for your negligence. You don't want to create more and more disappointment that your child will have for you.

Learn not to bad mouth each other in front of your child or make gestures that they have bad behaviors just like their Daddy or Mama. There is no perfect parent, and everyone is guilty of making mistakes. Words are powerful and will set in a child's memory for a lifetime. As they get older, they may be distant from you because of the hostile behavior they witnessed growing up. Children should never be torn against another parent. These types of attitudes could damage a child's self-esteem and could often play a role in how they relate to men or women in their adult life. Children tend to blame themselves for Mommy and Daddy not getting along, when it had nothing to do with them, it was their parent's decision. If you decide to take the high ground, and try to build a relationship to benefit Lebechi, it will be an easier road to travel for everyone to live happily ever after.

Chapter 8

Your Marriage Is What You Make It

Erin wants to get married, but her family and friends have put a deep fear in her heart, because the people in her life that were married, ended up getting a divorce. Her Mom and Dad, and Grandma and Grandpa got a divorce. Uncle Buck left Aunt Rita, and cousin Elroy got a divorce from her cousin Mary. Several of her family and friends talked down on commitment and true love, telling her not to believe the hype. Erin was told that people only got married for convenience. She constantly heard that men are dogs, and all that lovey-dovey hoopla is just a trap. Her heart was very stiff and guarded because she doesn't want to experience the hurt and pain she saw in her family.

Erin goes to the local coffee shop and unexpectedly meets a very nice guy. He shows much interest in her, but she repeatedly turns him down. He asked if she is married or a lesbian because she is treating him harsh. Jaleel was very persistent, and it is evident that he isn't going to give up. Erin finds out that they live in the same condominium complex near the coffee shop. She sees him again in the elevator and finally after much persuasion, she agrees to go on a date. Jaleel was funny, handsome, a freelance writer for a marketing firm and blogger with over two million followers. She has the absolute best time with him but continued to act uninterested.

Erin was used to being around guys, being the senior technical consultant with the New York Stock Exchange. They both have very successful careers, and very little time to enjoy the social life. After many months of dating, Jaleel starts asking Erin about her family. This is a subject that she would rather avoid because she knows there will be nothing but negativity once he meets them. His family lives in New Orleans and owns a chain of restaurants. He would often fly there to help the family but is following his own dreams of becoming a published author.

After dating a year, Erin flew from NYC to New Orleans to meet his family for the first time. His parents have been married for 30 years, older sisters and brothers have all been married for over 10 years, and they welcome her with open arms. Jaleel is the baby of the family, with two older sisters and two older brothers, in which three of them are happily married with children. Erin's whole outlook on marriage was slowly changing. The next few months, Erin finally opens up to Jaleel about her family and their negative views on marriage. He decided to still meet them because the relationship was becoming serious.

Erin constantly has nightmares about her family meeting Jaleel because they are very critical, and she doesn't know if this will make him run away from her. When Erin was a teenager her mom and dad got a divorce and her dad decided to remarry, but in his second marriage, he doesn't seem to be happy. Her dad got hurt on the job and is on disability, and her stepmom works full time to keep the bills paid. Erin feels that they aren't happy, just existing for convenience.

Erin's dad is very complacent and never seems to appreciate his wife. Her stepmom is always working and never takes the time to enjoy life and smell the roses. Erin loves her like a mom because she is so caring and always thinks of others. Erin hinted around to her dad to take her on a vacation, or out for a romantic dinner, but he always makes excuses about money. Erin decides to send her dad money to wine and dine her stepmom, because she is a good person and deserves it. Erin was so upset to find out through a family member that instead of treating her stepmom, her dad spends the money on fishing equipment, not even considering his wife's wants and needs. Erin wouldn't be surprised if one day, she receives a phone call to tell her that they are getting a divorce.

The day had finally come, and Erin and Jaleel flew to Oakland, California to meet her family. Erin has mixed emotions and wants to have a change of plans. She tells her mom and Grandma about him, and they decide they will be on their best behavior. They plan a family barbecue and invite the whole family to meet Erin's new boyfriend, Jaleel. Everyone treats him like family, cousins beat him in a game of dominoes, he wins chess and checkers, the ladies of the family all thought he was handsome and speak words of kindness.

Erin is on Cloud 9 and can't seem to stop smiling because she feels the love and acceptance. Her family tells her that they like him and only wants to see her happy. The next week, Erin gets a few calls from her cousins telling her that Jaleel was the talk of the entire weekend. Several of her cousins crowded the line on a three-way call saying, "He is like most guys, always seem to be nice and charming at the beginning but will quickly show their true faces once you are on lockdown." *Why does my family make marriage sound like prison?* Erin wondered.

"Marriage is a commitment, and some people have a happily ever after!" Erin yelled. She couldn't get this conversation out of her head because this is what she constantly dealt with in her family. Jaleel talked to Erin about making their relationship official. He was settled in his career and was ready to be a one-woman man. A few weeks later, Jaleel took her on a romantic getaway along Jersey shore and proposed to her on the beach. Erin was shocked, because she knew the relationship was headed in that direction, but after a year of dating she didn't realize he was ready for marriage so soon. When love comes knocking, will she answer?

Erin must realize that she is not her mom, Grandma, or any one of her other family members. There is nothing wrong with taking advice from loved ones, but their life doesn't have to be your life. You should not allow the hurt and pain your family experienced rub off on you. Jealousy and hurt can play a big part in the negativity of their thoughts of marriage. It is so unfortunate that your family has a curse of multiple divorces, but you can see that marriages can prosper by the longevity in your boyfriend's family. Stop listening to the naysayers, because misery loves company and marriage is between three people, you, your spouse, and God. There are problems within all marriages, but it doesn't have to end in divorce. No relationship is all sunshine, but two people can share one umbrella and survive the storm together.

Marriage helps you discover new dimensions within each other, some ups and downs but it is rewarding and truly beneficial to one's life. Pray together and keep God first. Learn to make your partner your number one priority, and keep your business your business, because everyone doesn't want to see you happy. Always communicate your feelings because problems will fester and get bigger if they go unresolved. Remember to pick your battles, every disagreement doesn't have to lead to an argument. Respect each other and love one another. A relationship takes the effort from both partners. If someone doesn't feel appreciated in the relationship, they may grow weary.

Always compliment your significant other and let them know that they are loved. Don't allow society to tell you when to show love and appreciation to your spouse. It doesn't have to be Valentine's Day, his or her birthday, or Christmas to enjoy gift giving. Pick up a bouquet of roses, take them dancing, go on a vacation getaway, or give them breakfast in bed. Acknowledgement and appreciation don't have to cost a lot of money. Assisting your spouse with taking out the trash, folding clothes, washing dishes, cooking a meal, or helping with the children can give you a lot of brownie points. Small tokens of affection and sweet gestures are just as special as big expensive gifts.

Your marriage is what you make it! Parents want the best for their children, but sometimes in life you must experience the rain to appreciate the rainbow. What won't hurt you will make you stronger. "As a man thinketh in his heart, so is he." **Proverbs 23:7**. Change your way of thinking and have faith. Life is about taking chances and learning through experiences. Keep the line of communication open, and always have God as the head of your lives. If you love him or her, make the commitment and although marriage is hard work, trust and believe that you will be married till death do you part.

India is known for its unique land of vibrant colors, breathtaking landscapes, and rich history. There are so many fun things to do in India such as, visiting the Taj Mahal, tiger safaris, an overnight stay on a backwater houseboat, close interactions with elephants, Himalaya skiing and camel rides in the desert. Prisha and Viraj grew up in the same village in India. They were friends in school and their families were very close. Prisha and Viraj enjoyed spending time together, and after high school, they both attended the same university. Their families decided once the two graduated, they would partake in an arranged marriage.

Prisha's Mom and Dad hinted around to their daughter of the idea, and she agreed but deep down she wanted to experience finding true love the American traditional way. Prisha had traveled to the United States as an exchange student, for a couple of years, and was amazed at how American women could freely choose the person they would spend the rest of their life with. Viraj loved Prisha and was ready to settle down with his longtime friend. He was so happy that their families were planning a big celebration, an arranged marriage. Prisha was gentle-hearted and cared more about other people's happiness rather than her own. She was afraid if she spoke up and didn't agree to the arranged marriage, that she would be a disappointment and damage the family's name. Prisha loved Viraj but wasn't in love with him. She loved him by habit because they grew up together. Prisha never imagined being romantic with Viraj, although he was very attractive, she never saw him in that way.

She told her mom about her feelings, explaining to her mom that she only liked Viraj as a friend, not a husband. She was told by her mom that she would grow to love him, because he is a good man and comes from a good family. Her Dad was so happy to soon be gaining a son, telling Prisha that Viraj would take good care of her. Graduation day was upon them, and the next weekend was the big celebration. Prisha couldn't truly enjoy obtaining her degree in nursing because she feared what was upon her, an arranged marriage. She was a people pleaser, she only majored in nursing because her family was filled with women nurses, and that's what her family encouraged her to major in, but she truly wanted to be a masseuse.

Prisha talked to Viraj about her feelings of not wanting to get married but remaining the best of friends. He accused her of just having cold feet. The big day had come, and she followed through with the ceremony, but wanted to scream inside because this wasn't the path she wanted for her life. She loved her Indian culture but felt that some of the women were too submissive and didn't possess any independence. Viraj was the happiest man alive, it was a beautiful ceremony! Prisha wasn't happy but decided to stay quiet to keep peace within the families. Many years had passed and Viraj had completed medical school and immediately received a job offer to a hospital in the United States. Prisha was ecstatic because she adored living in America. The couple moved to San Diego, California and Viraj allowed Prisha to pursue her dreams of becoming a masseuse.

Viraj was a wonderful provider for Prisha, but his work shift had him to spend very little time with her, which left her feeling neglected and vulnerable for outside attention. After many years of marriage, she still didn't feel that love spark that she was told she would eventually get by multiple women in her family. Prisha had so many clients asking for her within the agency. She loved giving her clients' massages, providing them with self-care, one day envisioning having her own company. Prisha and Viraj decided to start a family and was blessed with a beautiful baby girl named, Surashi. Prisha was so happy and hoped a new baby would help her have a change of heart and fall in love with her husband.

For many years, Prisha was faking her feelings for her husband, she knew he was a good catch, but not for her. After the baby was born, it seemed that Viraj and Prisha started to have more and more disagreements and silent treatments. They couldn't enjoy family time because Viraj was always working, even on his day off, he would be called for some type of medical emergency. Marriage issues was at an all-time high. Prisha truly regretted marrying Viraj, even before the career and the baby. She decided that they needed some space, so she gathered her personal belongings and moved to the east wing of the house, and he lived on the west wing. Sadly, Prisha not only wasn't in love with Viraj, but she also started not to have any love for him.

Viraj was an emotional wreck, he had work and relationship stress. He allowed his temper to get out of control one night and before he knew it, he had backhanded his wife, Prisha. She couldn't believe that her husband had put a bruise on her face. He had never been violent towards her, and this was the final straw. There was truly no relief for them because they didn't have any family in the states.

Prisha had a friend who was an attorney. She had been sharing with her what she was going through with her husband. After thorough research, and ten years of marriage, she filed for an official separation, but included visitation for him to see their daughter. Prisha was saddened but felt a freedom that she had been longing for, for many years. A few months later, one of her clients that she had admired for years came to her with a proposal that she couldn't refuse. She had been providing her client with facials and back massages for over five years and secretly had a crush on him. He was a widowed millionaire real estate broker and was Prisha's top client.

Mr. O'Hara was a white older American male, a very successful entrepreneur in the city. He had been featured on several nationwide business magazines. Mr. O'Hara presented Prisha with a property deed to start her own masseuse agency. She was so happy, especially when he granted her to own three locations in San Diego and two in Los Angeles. One of the locations foundations was already laid, because he wanted to prove to her how much he loved and cared for her. Mr. O'Hara explained to Prisha that he wanted her to be happy and do what she loved. Every location would have her own personal touch, as he agreed to help her create the blueprint. Mr. O'Hara assured Prisha that he would make her dream of becoming a business owner a reality, if only she marries him and make him a happy man. When love comes knocking, will she answer?

Many cultures have their own way that they celebrate their heritage. There are many successful arranged marriages in the world, however, Prisha expressed her desire to be able to get married the traditional American way at the very beginning. Her family persuaded her to participate in the arranged marriage because it was what was expected in their Indian culture.

You love your family, and they truly want the best for you, but they must allow you to follow your own path. No one was truly listening to Prisha's cry for help and because she never was able to make her own decisions for her life, she went along with the marriage and her family's career choice for her. No matter how attractive a person may be or family they were born into, you cannot fake love. Eventually the truth will present itself.

Viraj was sincere about his feelings for Prisha, but her feelings weren't mutual. It takes two people to make a marriage work. When problems arise in a marriage, it doesn't matter if your location changes and a baby is involved, unless the person has a change of heart, the root of the problem is still present, and it may make matters worse. Stress will make a person act out of character and do things that they wouldn't normally do. However, no one should tolerate any physical or verbal abuse in a relationship.

Sadly, Prisha is preparing to end a marriage that shouldn't have never happened. The two of them should have remained only best friends. Mr. O'Hara had been flirting with Prisha for a while, even before her marriage was in jeopardy, and she secretly admired him. The proposal to her from Mr. O'Hara sounds very promising, but how much does she really know about this millionaire real estate broker? Is she in love with Mr. O'Hara or does she love the opportunity that he can give her? Everything that glitters isn't gold. Money solves a lot of problems but doesn't bring you happiness. Let's hope Prisha makes the best decision for her and her daughter.

Chapter 9

When Love Complicates Life

Amber is the daughter of a very prestigious cheese powerhouse from Green Bay, Wisconsin. Her family's business started many years ago and has gone international, exporting cheese to Italy and Japan. They are often featured in many national publications. Amber is constantly involved with the marketing of her family business, and as her dad gets older, he plans to pass down the torch to her and her siblings.

Amber is so busy with the business that her love life has suffered. She goes online and visits some of the dating websites, reading the reviews, and decides to enter her profile. She doesn't put anything specific to her profession because she doesn't want anyone to show interest because of her wealthy family. It takes a few days, and she finally starts to get a few hits. There were some interesting guys, however, Amber is just doing it for fun. Her life is very busy with the business, but she wants to let her hair down a little.

Amber connects with a guy name Bradford that seems to have a similar background as hers, working in his family business on a farm. They decided to chat together and agreed not to talk about their careers, but just focus on hobbies and other things that make them happy. Amber discusses past relationships, traveling, and reading good books. After a few weeks of chatting, Amber decides to meet Bradford for dinner.

She was very happy that he looked exactly like his profile picture. He seemed to be smitten with her as well. There's an instant connection between the both of them, but their lives are always consumed with work, so they both decide that work won't be a topic of discussion. The relationship had been going strong for four months now, and neither had discussed meeting each other families.

Amber has already imagined their lives together, seeing their wedding invitation with their names Bradford and Amber. Bradford mentioned taking Amber on a romantic weekend getaway and she was thrilled. They arrived at the resort and as they entered the restaurant, Amber notices that they are getting a few stares. The owner of the restaurant comes to the table to greet the two of them, while acting a little weird.

He is very familiar with Amber and her family's business but seems a bit disturbed by her date's presence. As the night comes to an end, her prince charming, Bradford tells her that he is falling in love with her and is ready to meet each other's families. Amber finally gets up the nerve to tell her parents about Bradford, the new guy in her life, and when they ask about his career, Amber blurts out, "He works with his family on their farm."

As Bradford picks her up, Amber sees that he is such a gentleman. He is prepared to present a gift to her family. It is wrapped so eloquently, and Amber is excited because she knows he will make a good impression. Bradford greets her mom with a hug and presents the gift to her. He shakes hands with her dad, and they both seemed pleased. After dinner, Bradford announces that the gift was specifically made by his family.

As Amber's Mom opens the gift, it is a beautiful gourmet gift basket of sausage, cheese, crackers, and wine, but what was very surprising, it was from the family's competitor! Bradford's family business is true Wisconsin cheese rivals of Amber's family's cheese business. They are both members of the WCMA, Wisconsin Cheese Makers Association, but because Amber and Bradford works behind the scenes in marketing and accounting and never really discussed work, the two didn't know their families were rivals. When love comes knocking, will they answer?

When you are in a relationship, it is always best to have open communication and ask as many questions as possible, that way you can decide whether you want to invest your time in the relationship. Amber is falling in love with the son of a competitor, but it is not the end of the world. Bradford's feelings are mutual for Amber and although their families are rivals, it may only be a friendly competition. This situation will be complicated, but you must decide if you can make it work.

The restaurant owner looked disturbed by both being in the company of each other because they are competitors, but because they never fully discussed their careers, they had no knowledge of what was going on. A part of getting to know each other better is to know each other's backgrounds, passions, hobbies, and career choices. Always have effective communication and be flexible with any situation. If the love between the two of you is strong enough, you and your families can find a way to separate the personal from the professional.

Mia and Jose have been dating for about nine months. Mia is a registered nurse for the local hospital, and Jose is a licensed mechanic and just opened a new shop of his own. They both have had long-term relationships in the past and is ready to start a new life together. One day Mia visits Jose at his apartment and when she goes to the bathroom, she decided to snoop around in his medicine cabinet and found several medications for treating symptoms of STDs.

She wondered if they are his, but he doesn't have a roommate. Mia is totally shocked and disappointed because the two of them have been talking about taking their relationship to the next level. How does she approach Jose with her findings? How will she admit to him about her nosey ways? Jose has asked Mia what type of diamond ring she would like. He wants to marry her and has been hinting around to ask her dad for her hand in marriage. Will Mia ask Jose about his medications? When love comes knocking, will she answer?

Did you know there are millions of new STD cases in the United States each year, and millions of people living with ongoing sexually transmitted diseases? Mia should admit to her findings, and ask if the medication belongs to him, before walking down the aisle of commitment. Jose must be open and honest about anything that may jeopardize the relationship. The two of you should want to have a clean slate and be comfortable enough to admit your imperfections. If he admits to taking the medication to cure an STD, be open about your feelings, ask questions and take your time to decide. If Jose is sick, he should have addressed this to you immediately. When you are in a committed relationship, you should be able to trust your significant other wholeheartedly.

Having good health, trust and honesty, financial stability, strong faith, love, and respect all make up good qualities for having a strong lasting relationship. You can still live a happy and healthy life being HIV positive, with the right medical care, eating nutritious meals, and exercise. After everything has been revealed, it should give you the answer that you need to decide if you will continue the relationship or move forward. Your decision will affect the rest of your life. Take your time and make your decisions rationally. Do not rush into anything, because a long-lasting relationship cannot function on distrust. Keep communicating and listening and know that health is wealth. Seek ongoing treatment, get tested, and make decisions that will be in your best interest.

Farrah is a naturally born shopaholic! Although she likes to shop on a budget, her happy place is buying for herself and everyone else. She doesn't have to get a gift in return, she just likes to shop. Farrah has had to pay bills late because she constantly overspends, but because she is single, it doesn't appear to be a problem for her. She splurges on buying designer handbags that cost close to what she pays in rent. Farrah doesn't save because she wants to cherish every day like it is her last. She is horrible with money, and her credit score is constantly decreasing because she is steadily falling behind on making payments.

Farrah desperately needs some financial help, but she feels she is too deep in debt. She pays her bank insufficient fund fees because she is not budgeting properly. Her company is having a retirement and financial planning seminar and she plans to attend. Farrah is happy that she can go to the seminar and get some much-needed information. A financial representative agrees to meet with her over lunch to go over her own individual accounts. The next week, Farrah receives a phone call to tell her that the financial planner is sending his business partner because he had a schedule conflict.

She meets with his business partner and is in total shock. What she didn't know was that her ex-boyfriend Paul, who she lost contact with, is a partner with the financial consulting firm. Her business luncheon turns into a date with an old flame. Farrah never really discusses her finances because she is too busy playing catch up on things she's missed over the years. When they dated in the past, they were both young and made bad choices when it came to the relationship. They are much older and wiser now and seemed to be so happy that they've reunited. They are both single with no children and is exploring the possibility of rekindling their love. Farrah still has this heavy debt hanging over her head but continues to shop and overspend. Over the months, Farrah and her newfound love Paul have become closer and closer. He is happy to tell his sister, who was once her close friend that the two of them are back together again.

Paul assures Farrah that he won't let her get away again. After three months of dating, Farrah is fearful that if she opens up about her debt, the relationship will end. She is constantly drowning in debt, no savings account, credit cards are maxed out, she has insufficient funds on her bank accounts, and owes over $100,000 on her student loans. She is so ashamed of her immature spending habits but can't admit it to Paul. One day Paul's sister calls Farrah to tell her that her brother cannot wait to give her his last name. Farrah is desperately in need of professional help. When love comes knocking, will she answer?

This is very sticky, because Farrah knows that she has a problem and continues to get herself in deeper debt. It may be beneficial to communicate to her ex-boyfriend, now boyfriend Paul of her financial problems. He is an expert, and it is better to discuss it now than waiting until the two of you become closer in love. God may have blessed the both of you to cross paths to help save you from the continued stresses you are dealing with from overspending. You are making a great salary, but because of your lack of budgeting and managing money, it has caused you to lose thousands of dollars.

They always say it is not the money that you make but what you can keep. In marriages there are ups and downs, why not get some of the downs out of the way and tell Paul about your problems? He should know now how much debt you are in, because if the relationship gets serious and you consider marriage, he will inherit your debt. You never know why things happen in life. You have been praying to get your finances in order and get the help you desperately need. Tell your truth and start a new beginning with the one you love debt free.

Chapter 10

You Did Not Marry Your Daddy

Rylee meets a guy, and it is an instant love at first sight. Samuel is the exact opposite of Rylee, but they fit together like a puzzle piece. The two cannot get enough of each other. She is falling in love with Samuel, but he is 20 years older than her, and has some old school ways that she doesn't know if she can deal with. Samuel doesn't seem to like the same interest as her, and when the two of them double date with her friends, he seems to be bored out of his mind.

Samuel treats Rylee like a queen, and he constantly talks about marriage but never about children. Rylee doesn't know if it is because he is a lot older than her that he doesn't want children or just never mentions it. As a woman in her early 30's, her biological clock is ticking, and she is patiently waiting but doesn't want to wait too long. One day Samuel's ex-girlfriend Ariana approaches her to let her know that they are going to have a baby together. Rylee feels betrayed because he told her that the relationship had been over many years ago. When she confronted him about it, he tells her that Ariana is jealous and is trying to create a situation between the two of them.

Rylee wants to believe him, but in the back of her mind, she doesn't know what to do if the baby were his. He assured her that he doesn't love Ariana anymore, and that she can't stand the fact that he has someone else. After constant arguments about his ex, Samuel tells Rylee that he is 100% sure that the baby is not his because he never slept with her, and he cannot have children, due to a terrible batting accident he had on his little league team when he was seven. Although Rylee is relieved that he may not be the father, she is in total shock that her future husband won't be able to produce children. When love comes knocking, will she answer?

The two of you grew up in totally different generations, but it doesn't mean it can't work. There are a lot of couples with a big age difference and their marriages are thriving. You must learn to see the beauty in each other's interest. Maybe decide to do something Rylee likes one weekend, and what Samuel likes the next. You don't want to seem like you are dating your Daddy, so if it is too complicated to handle, maybe having a friendship will suffice. It is always important to have discussions about your future with your potential mate. If the situation had never occurred with his ex-girlfriend Ariana approaching you, will you have ever known about his infertility issues?

Samuel should have communicated about his batting accident to you early in the relationship. When you don't speak up about a situation it causes confusion. If you are unable to produce children, it is not the end of the world, but it is a very important factor and should not be taken lightly. You may not mind, because there are always options like adopting a child, caring for a foster child, or having a surrogate. Try and be considerate of his feelings and be open-minded because it is very hard for anyone to admit their lack of anything. Make sure to analyze the situation thoroughly and if you are meant to be together, everything else will fall in place. Take time to love beyond the top of the surface, dig deep, communicate, and ask questions.

Evan has retired from the U.S. Army and is looking for love again because his first wife passed away from cancer. He suffers from Post-Traumatic Stress Disorder (PTSD), which causes him to frequently have images and nightmares about certain disturbing things he has encountered while serving in the military. After having weekly meetings with his psychologist, Evan has been prescribed medications.

Evan has lost a leg while in combat, which now has him disabled. He wants to find someone special that will accept him for all his flaws. He meets a lady named Vivian through a mutual friend. She is very nice, comes from a military family, and is very familiar with being disabled. Her Dad served in World War II and lost his arm. The two of them go on several dates and he loves the way she shows him love and respect, although he knows it is hard to deal with an amputee.

After many months of dating, Evan and his buddies hang out and he tells them that Vivian is "The One." Evan has met her family and she has met his. The only problem is she wants him to get a prosthetic leg because of his appearance of not having a leg isn't pleasing to her. He has adjusted to having one leg for many years, before even meeting her. As he attempts to have a conversation with her about not getting a prosthetic leg, she referenced her dad because he got a prosthetic arm a few years after the war. This has been a constant battle with the two of them. Many arguments have surrounded this issue. Evan loves her but she can't seem to accept him fully. This is the only issue that seems to be stopping Evan from asking her to marry him. When love comes knocking, will he answer?

Evan is healthy and nothing is stopping him from living a happy, retired, stress-free life, so Vivian should be supportive of him. As little girls we love our Daddy's, they can't do any wrong in our eyes. They are our first man crushes, our loves, and we tend to compare our significant others to them. Let's face reality, we are not in a committed relationship with our dads.

You should never expect your boyfriend, fiancé, or husband to do everything like your dad, so don't have this as an expectation, because you will be let down, and it will cause complications in your relationship. Vivian seems to be caught up in what everyone around her may think. What if Evan asked Vivian to be like his mom? It isn't fair to expect someone to be like someone else because hopefully you fell in love with them for who they are, not for who you hope for them to be. If your boyfriend isn't complaining about his disability, then you shouldn't either. Don't allow anyone to disturb your peace, talk to her and hopefully she will understand your point of view. Remember she isn't marrying her Daddy.

Don't be so concerned about what people may say or think. Evan doesn't want to get a prosthetic leg. He is happy and laid down his life for our country, so you may want to let this topic rest, if not, your nagging ways will make Evan want to distance himself from you. It is not easy for veterans to adapt to civilian life after retiring. Some veterans go through difficult periods, making it harder to adjust, while some find their new roles in society fulfilling.

Veterans returning to the work force may have a period of catch up, learning new skills, or adjusting to a new position. This may also include adjusting to some social changes that may have occurred in the workplace. Some veterans may also suffer from worry of job loss or may have some mental health challenges. If you are dealing with a similar issue, be supportive and encouraging because this is what he or she needs. They have been very courageous in serving in the military, so support is needed in getting back to civilian life. Vivian should not let her selfish ways corrupt a potentially good relationship. To all the men and women fighting for our country, many thanks for your service, you are highly appreciated!

Chapter 11

Games Are for Kids

Donald is an executive for an oil and gas company, and he loves what he does. He has been working in the oil and gas industry for over 15 years and his fiancé is reaping the benefits of his hard work. Irene owns her own boutique in the Galleria, and it is very profitable, keeping her just as busy. Donald is always swamped in his work that he occasionally brings it home. Irene, his fiancé is not fond of the work he brings along, which includes his secretary.

Sometimes when Irene comes home late, Donald and his secretary Sasha are enjoying a meal together without her. Donald swears up and down that there is nothing going on, it is only business. Irene feels differently because Sasha wears very sexy and revealing clothing. Irene is upset that Donald seemed so naïve, as if he never noticed her sexy attire. Sasha acted cordial and respectful in front of Irene, but behind closed doors, she doesn't know what to think.

If Donald doesn't bring his work home, he may often stay at work late. Sasha sometimes picks up his breakfast, rearranges his office, and makes dinner reservations for the two of them to discuss business. It is what most assistants does, but Irene can't seem to stop being suspicious of their relationship. Irene wanted to believe Donald, but his assistant doesn't have family in the area, and doesn't have a man of her own. Every business trip Sasha tags along, staying in the same hotel but different hotel rooms, but the two of them often share meals and enjoy sightseeing together. Donald sees the pain this relationship with his secretary is causing Irene but isn't changing his actions.

Irene has caught Donald in the past being unfaithful, she forgave him and although she believes him now, there is still a small percentage telling her that "he wants his cake and eat it too." Irene has a very demanding and successful boutique business, selling high end fashions and is unable to travel with him. She has constantly told Donald about her concerns, and he assured her that nothing is going on. He explained to Irene that he loved her unconditionally and was ready to make her his wife, not his assistant. When love comes knocking, will she answer?

You cannot have a marriage without trust. Irene must have a sit-down talk about some boundaries that should be taken when it comes to Donald and his secretary. Work should be kept at work, and if it carries over, his secretary should be given specific instructions on how to complete her task independently at the office or her own home. It seems that business and pleasure is being mixed, and they are both denying any wrongdoings. If the shoe were on the other foot, and Irene's business partner were a man, coming home with her sharing meals together without her fiancé, I don't think this would be tolerated. If someone treats you like an option, you may have to leave them by choice. Relationships should always have honesty and respect, and this one seems to be lacking a lot of it. You have witnessed firsthand some behaviors from your fiancé that you have addressed, but he continues not to listen.

At some point your work should be cut off to spend quality time with the one you love. You must have trust and understanding, and if you are unable to communicate your likes and dislikes, this will be the beginning of a bad relationship. Continue to let your fiancé know how the set-up is affecting you and your relationship with him. Ask him to seek pre-marital counseling from a minister or marriage counselor. If the relationship is important to him, he will make the necessary adjustments to make it work and build up the trust again to live a happy life together.

Brantley is a loving husband from Charlotte, North Carolina who lives with his wife and two boys. He loves his family immensely, but the world of temptation surrounds him. He is a truck driver, on a mission to one day have his own trucking company. Brantley travels across the United States, and although he keeps love for his wife in his heart, his heart gets weak and lonely, and he allows his flesh to speak. Brantley loved God and his family, but he has grown apart from God because of the hardships of his life, being without a father, and the death of his mom and Grandma. He was raised in the church and often read the Bible with his Grandma but have grown cold towards God.

Most of his truck buddies are single, and the ones that are married, are very unhappy and have extra marital affairs. Brantley sees the drama in their lives, but falls in the very same trap, making excuses for not coming home to his family, and one lie turns into another and another. His wife Whitney became a bride at an early age, and never had a career of her own. He has always been the breadwinner of the family, and although the bills are paid, and he makes sure her and the boys have spending money, he is always making excuses not to come and spend quality family time at home.

The marriage is failing, and Whitney has expressed to him repeatedly that she is not happy. His absence is truly hurting the family. Whitney struggles with her boys, because she is doing everything by herself, it is truly like she is a single parent. Brantley is so caught up in his own pleasures that he fails to realize that his marriage will soon be over. The two of them have been married for 18 years and because of Brantley's selfish ways, he has allowed the enemy to end what God had put together. He slowly starts with one affair, that mistress thinks she is the leading lady, until he tells her that he is married, and she tells him that she is pregnant. Before you know it, he has so many women and babies popping up all over the United States in different area codes. Brantley cannot believe the mess he has created, and the hurt he has caused his family.

Surprisingly, he is served with divorce papers and child support orders at the same time from his wife and his mistresses. Brantley starts slacking on the job and multiple deliveries doesn't make it to their destination on time. He has gotten several warnings for texting while driving, and many speeding tickets. His mistresses call several times within the week, leaving harassing threats to him and making demands on the company's voicemail. He loses his job because of the distractions in his life.

Brantley continues to be in and out of court because of the women that he decided to impregnate. He is now the father of six children, two boys with his wife, and four others with his mistresses. His life is filled with drama, hurt, and disappointment. Brantley's own siblings are so ashamed of the choices he has made for his life. He was their role model, being the oldest of five children after losing their parents to heart disease. Brantley had to file for bankruptcy, was homeless for years, but was determined to get his life back on track.

He had a happy and peaceful life when he was with his wife and boys. He had love, trust, peace, and prosperity. Brantley got hurt on the job years before he got terminated and won the wrongful injury lawsuit. It is now five years later, and Brantley reaches out to his ex-wife Whitney and their two boys. He had never been a good dad to them, even before the infidelity. He never attended any of their swim meets or theatrical performances, always making false promises. Brantley wants to be back in their lives for good, and although they are grown men in college, he wants their forgiveness and love back.

Brantley's ex-wife Whitney is an administrative assistant for an engineering firm and loves her new life. She is single and happy with her cute little Yorkie dog, Roxie, occasional happy hour with her girlfriends, and volunteers with the youth group at her church. Brantley has driven thousands of miles to show up to his ex-wife's job and confess his love to her, with a bouquet of roses and dinner reservations, in front of her co-workers. When he arrives, he practically begs her for a little bit of her time, the same time that she begged him to spend with her and their boys for nearly 18 years.

Brantley's entire life has changed for the better. He is a proud owner of his own trucking company worth millions, owner of real estate in Alabama, Mississippi, Georgia, Texas, and Ohio, and assures his ex-wife Whitney that she won't ever have to struggle again. Brantley asked her to help him run the company. He also asked her to forgive him and consider taking him back. Brantley surprised Whitney with the keys to a brand-new house that he had secretly built for her in Ohio. This is dear to her because it was built on the land owned by her ancestors. He gave her the keys to the Range Rover that he picked her up in, agreed to go to marriage counseling, has a closer relationship with God, and has gotten back in church and serves with the usher ministry.

Brantley shared with Whitney that he wanted a second chance to love her the way that she is meant to be loved. He asked God for forgiveness, and prayed to him to get his wife back, because he wants to do what is right. Whitney enjoyed dinner with Brantley, laughing and reminiscing about old times, but kept getting distracted because of the text messages and phone calls he was receiving from his mistresses. When love comes knocking, will she answer?

Sadly, Brantley had to hit rock bottom to realize what mattered the most in his life. Whitney had been married to Brantley for 18 years, her high school sweetheart, who didn't honor his commitment to her, their family and God. Everyone is entitled to make mistakes, but the suffering she endured raising her boys practically alone can never be changed. You must decide whether you want to continue to enjoy your life in peace and happiness, or give him another chance to get it right, but you may always be wondering if he is being truthfully faithful. Are you comfortable with having a relationship with the extended family? You must truly understand that it is no longer you and the boys he will have to take care of, but your family and many other families. He is the father of your two boys, two girls and two more boys between the ages of four and sixteen, with four other mothers.

Do you know what his relationship is like with his children's mothers, and with his other children? Your sons are bitter towards their dad, because of his lack of being present in their lives. Although you and the boys should discuss forgiving Brantley, your life is drama free, but if you become one with him again, his problems will become your problems. The text messages and phone calls won't stop if you give him another chance but get worse. You must realize that he has other obligations besides you and your family. Your life is perfect in every way. You rest peacefully at night, your boys are great students, and constantly on the Dean's list in college. You are active in your church, you have girlfriends to go out with occasionally, a beautiful condominium, great job as an administrator, although it doesn't pay much, but you aren't lacking in anything.

Are you open to re-marrying your ex-husband? It is awesome that Brantley has gotten a closer relationship with God and worked so hard to turn his life around. It seems that he is a much better man and truly wants to start all over with you. Listen and know the facts. You shouldn't be so quick to make any changes not knowing the specifics. You must weigh the pros and cons of the situation and decide if you are willing to relocate from North Carolina to Ohio to help run your ex-husband's businesses. Are you ready to have a relationship with his four children and their four mothers? Make sure you are not creating any distractions for your boys and get them off course from doing their best in school. Remember to put your wants and needs first, pray, and consider what you are giving up before making any hasty decisions that will change your life for better or worse.

Chapter 12

A Family That Prays Together Stays Together

Ada believes in God, but her family's work schedule prohibited her from going to church every Sunday as a child. In her adult life, she was content with watching TV church, but attended church on Mother's Day, Easter, and Christmas. Ada uses work as an excuse for not going to church with Eddie but working on Sundays is not mandatory. As a child, Ada only attended church regularly when she went with her Grandma during the summer.

She meets a man named Eddie through a mutual friend that is a member of a gospel quartet, serves on the church board of trustees, plays the guitar and drums, a faithful member of Bible study and Sunday school and sings in the adult traveling choir. Eddie absolutely loved participating in church activities. This is what he experienced growing up with his parents, and he wants Ada to join him in his love of fellowship and worship. Eddie and Ada have been dating for over a year, she loves him, and he loves her. Eddie is a very attractive man and always turns heads everywhere he goes.

Ada works from home and uses the excuse that she has projects to do for work to not attend church. She is often too busy to pray with Eddie, always using work or anything she can think of as an excuse. Ada has unconsciously given up on God, because she believes that he took a lot of her family members away. There are a lot of single ladies at the church that constantly flirts with her boyfriend Eddie. He loves Ada and only Ada, but he is human, and the temptation is real.

Eddie expresses to Ada how he wants her to share his love and attend church services, because her presence and support would help him fight off the single ladies. It would help build strength to the relationship and show his church members that he is taken. Eddie comes home with cakes, cookies, and pies from his admirers.

Ada seemed to enjoy the sweet treats just as much as Eddie without a care in the world. He has received gifts in the mail, and he can't believe how upfront these ladies tend to be with their lustful ways. Although he tells them he has a special lady, no one has seen her in the present. Eddie has prayed about the situation, because he wants to make Ada his wife, and has plans to propose to her through a song at one of his church musicals, but she continues to make excuses to not come, and he is not sure if she will ever be in attendance.

Ada wants to get married and become Eddie's wife, even hinting around about a wedding date. He wants to discuss his concerns with his pastor and possibly start pre-marital counseling, but Ada is against it, because she doesn't want anyone in her business. Eddie loves Ada but her lack of support and nonchalant behavior about her faith and spirituality is weighing heavily on him, and now he is questioning if she is truly meant for him. There are a lot of decisions to be made. When love comes knocking, will he answer?

Eddie, were you not aware of her wayward faith and spirituality before or after you met her? Ada, did you not know about his strong faith in God and love for the ministry? There seems to be a lack of communication within this relationship, or the two are assuming they can change each other's ways. Your expectations of each other should be communicated early in the relationship. If you don't have effective communication, it will pose a problem. Eddie loves his church and all the ministries that he is a part of. He wants to share his love with Ada and have her right by his side. This is not too much to ask for, especially since her work schedule on Sunday is not mandatory. It sounds like Ada is making an excuse to not get up and get dressed to go and worship at church, because she is so content with watching TV church.

Love is about compromising, and it wouldn't hurt to support him in doing what he loves to do, and he supports her in what makes her happy. Women are always complaining about there are no good men out there, or they are unable to get their man to go to church. Ada has been warned by her boyfriend that the ladies are waiting in line because he is a good catch, and because they hear about Ada, but haven't seen her face, they will continue with their flirtatious ways.

Don't lose a good man over cakes, cookies, and pies, because he may start gravitating toward the ones that share his interests and pleases his stomach. Make sure there is no one else in her life. Ada doesn't seem startled one bit by the extra attention Eddie is receiving at church. If she wants the relationship to work, she must start out by supporting him, worship with other believers, and hearing a good word from God, it is great medicine for the soul. Ada may find out that she likes it enough to start participating in one of the ministries. Make sure before both of you walk down the aisle, you seek pre-marital counseling.

Read the Bible together, pray together and open a discussion with Ada about losing her loved ones, this may be the root cause of her avoiding worshipping and praying with you. It is hard but you cannot change people, they must want to change, and if she doesn't see that there is a problem, you will continue to have discourse in your relationship. Your faith in God and love for praise and worship is what gives you strength and you want to share it with the one you love. Express to her the joy and happiness it will make you feel if she accompanies you, she just may enjoy it herself. Pray and ask for God's direction.

Chloe is dating Cameron a guy that comes from a huge family. She met him at a community outreach event five years ago in Atlanta. His parents were blessed with 10 handsome boys that have grown into successful young men. They are the proud grandparents of 15 grandchildren.

From oldest to youngest sons, Jordan is a psychologist, Tyler is an engineer, Bryson is an attorney, Christian is a primary care physician, Isaiah is an entrepreneur, Logan is a meteorologist, Grant is a professional basketball player, Aiden is a military sergeant, Noah is an airplane pilot, and her boyfriend Cameron, is a substitute teacher, who is aspiring to be a high school math teacher but can't seem to pass the content exam.

Cameron is the baby of the family, and some of the family seems to show him no respect because of his inconsistencies of what he wants to do in his life. One day he wants to go to the Atlanta Police Academy, to be in law enforcement. He quickly changes his mind after he witnessed his childhood friend being taunted by an officer. He volunteered a lot in the community, so he decided to be a community activist, until one day a situation occurred, and he sees his life flash before his eyes.

He feels like he was born to give back, now he is pursuing teaching. Cameron has always been an above average student, and graduated from college with honors, but still struggles to find his niche in life. His girlfriend Chloe is his #1 fan, always encouraging him to pray and ask God to reveal his purpose in life. She is a pediatrician at Emory Hospital in Atlanta and visualizes having a baby of her own one day, but because of her endometriosis, she doesn't know if her dream will become a reality.

Mama Claire, Cameron's mother adores all nine of her daughter-in-law's, including Chloe. They are so close, because she always wanted girls, and God blessed her with nine daughters-in-law's that she calls her daughters. They have brunch together, weekend getaways, members of the same book club, and attends the same church. Chloe, Cameron's girlfriend is very close to his family, but doesn't see them that often because of her work schedule.

Everything about Cameron's family seems so perfect and she doesn't know how she and Cameron will measure up because of his career instability and her health issues. One day surprisingly, Chloe gets a call from Mama Claire to join her and the other daughters-in-law on a cruise a few months away. Chloe checked her schedule to see that she has some flexibility to take a week off. She was so excited that she and the ladies will enjoy some much-needed relaxation time in Cancun, Mexico.

Chloe and Cameron can't wait to make their relationship official, but he wants to pass his test and get a teaching job first. Chloe enjoys the trip but feels a little left out when they are discussing their children. Some of her soon to be sisters-in-law seem to love attention and tries to compete on gift giving during special occasions for their in-laws.

Chloe doesn't want to be a part of any competition, because she saw it a lot growing up in her own family. One day Chloe makes a quick visit to Everly's house, her soon to be sister-in-law. She was asked to drop off a copy of her daughter's birth certificate. Everly asked her for a copy of the birth certificate because she didn't feel like going to the courthouse and Chloe is her daughter's pediatrician.

Chloe arrived to Everly's house earlier than expected and noticed her boyfriend's other brother Tyler's car is in the driveway. She doesn't think anything of it because they are all very close. She rings the doorbell, but no one comes to the door. When Chloe goes back to her car that is parked down the street, she sees Everly come out and look around, then kisses her brother-in-law Tyler goodbye on the lips in a very intimate way. "Oh, my goodness!" Chloe lets out a silent scream while sitting in her car. "What is happening here?" She asked herself. She is totally shocked.

Chloe is so upset because Everly has been married to the other brother Noah, the airplane pilot for many years. She is so nervous because she doesn't know what to do. She wants to immediately say something to her boyfriend Cameron but doesn't know the whole story, only what she saw. Thankfully she was parked near a tree so far down that no one saw her. After playing the scene again and again in her head, she finally got the courage to tell Cameron about his brother Tyler and sister-in-law Everly. She tells Cameron and he is beyond angry! He starts to reminisce on all the times Tyler has belittled him and his career choices. Cameron is ready to confront his brother, but Chloe swears him to secrecy until the time is right.

One Sunday after church service everyone is at the in-laws eating a family dinner when Cameron surprisingly proposes to Chloe! Cameron explains that his life isn't perfect, but he loves her and can't stand to wait any longer to become Mr. and Mrs. Everyone is amazed and clapped in excitement for the newly engaged couple. Mama Claire is so excited and makes a toast as she will soon welcome a new daughter to the family.

Tyler spoiled the mood and confronted Cameron about his career. He does it in a very nagging way, trying to embarrass him in front of the family. Grant, Isaiah, and Jordan are upset that Tyler is ruining the couple's happy moment. Mr. Eugene, the father of the family, is very soft spoken but decided to keep his house in order and asked the boys to settle down, because the argument was beginning to escalate. Tyler continued to degrade Cameron in his lack of career goals.

Cameron decided to take the high ground and was getting ready to leave, but Tyler wouldn't stop with his nagging. Cameron decided to blurt out to the family about the request Everly made to his fiancé Chloe for a copy of their daughter Kennedy's birth certificate. He spoke up about Chloe arriving early and witnessed Tyler and Everly engaging in a passionate kiss. Tyler's wife is Hannah and Everly is married to Noah, the airplane pilot who is never at home. Everyone was in total shock! Mama Claire asked Cameron to sit down and demanded Tyler to confess if it was true. Tyler wouldn't speak, he just stared at Cameron in disbelief. Tyler asked his wife Hannah to leave with him, but she refused and was waiting on a response.

Everly started talking about she had been living with a secret for 3 years and needed to come clean. She confessed that she and Tyler had a crush on each other since high school, but because Tyler was in a relationship, she and Noah started dating, but her feelings never left for Tyler. After a football game they met up, and one thing led to another, and she and Tyler had sex. Everly confessed that her daughter Kennedy is not Tyler's niece, but his daughter. Everyone's jaw dropped in disbelief. The entire room was silenced. Suddenly, a roar of loud screaming, yelling, cursing, and crying; the house was filled with emotions! Chloe didn't realize it until the argument happened that Noah signed the birth certificate, even though Everly knew that Tyler was the father.

Noah was on a flight and scheduled to be home the next week. The yelling and screaming carried on for a while when Mr. Eugene demanded that everyone settle down. Hannah, Tyler's wife begins to cry. Mama Claire consoled her while staring at her son Tyler. Hannah couldn't believe how many times her and Everly had hung out enjoying spa days together, having play dates with their children, and couple's movie nights when Noah was in town. "Why did you do this to me Tyler?" Hannah asked. The brothers, Jordan, Logan, Bryson, Christian, Isaiah, Aiden, and Grant shook their heads in shame and remained speechless.

It was so sad that the perfect family, wasn't so perfect anymore. Sunday dinners will never be the same. Chloe had been waiting for the day to be able to enjoy planning her wedding with her mother-in-law and sister-in-law's. Cameron and Chloe love each other dearly, but with the family going through a big mess, is it the right time to make their love official and make wedding plans? When love comes knocking, will they answer?

There is no problem that doesn't have a solution. After dating for five years and engaged to your best friend, it is time to celebrate. No one is perfect, and there is no such thing as the perfect family. You are marrying each other, you will be in the family, but not marrying the entire family. The two of you should decide when would be a good time to make wedding plans. It is very unfortunate that some of your families have been deceitful and untrustworthy, but you can't put your lives on hold because of the mess they have created. Although you should be empathetic to your family during this difficult time, because you want them to enjoy the love and happiness between the two of you.

Hopefully Cameron's family can have effective communication and possibly counseling to get back on the right track. It is sad that Noah will return home to a life-changing situation, but don't let it steal your joy. Everly should never have dated Noah because she continued to have feelings for his brother Tyler. Tyler should have been open with his brother Noah about his crush on Everly, but because of their secrets, it has caused strife within the family. The saddest part of this story is that there is an innocent little three-year-old girl that will one day have to be told that her uncle is actually her Daddy. Use this situation to make sure there is always open communication in your marriage. When someone is not truthful about their feelings and actions, it causes problems.

Having a spouse that works out of town often makes it easy for your partner to have temptations, but it is not an excuse to cheat, especially with a family member. You must have self-discipline. Effective communication, love, respect, honesty, and prayer is the key to keeping a lasting and loving relationship. Chloe shouldn't feel guilty about what she witnessed that day, because what is done in the dark will surely come to the light. The birth certificate request was an outlet to eventually finding out their dirty little secret. When Noah returns home, the marriage may be rocky or may end, but hopefully he will be able to forgive his wife and brother and continue to provide love and care to his daughter-niece Kennedy.

Piper and Darnell rekindled their friendship at their 20th high school class reunion. They were good friends throughout high school but had lost contact for many years. Darnell was a retired Master Sergeant in the United States Marine Corp and Piper was a licensed daycare owner. Darnell's children are teenagers 13 and 15, and Piper's children are 3 and 5. Darnell grew up in a strict two-parent home and believed in giving children their bare necessities, love, and discipline.

Piper's beliefs were totally different than Darnell, she believed that children should be open to express themselves even if it comes across as disrespectful. After three months of dating, the two decided it was time to meet each other's children. They both felt that the relationship was going to another level. Darnell brought his 15-year-old son and 13-year-old daughter to the restaurant. They were very polite, only spoke when spoken to, and his son was a gentleman, often opening the door for the females that entered the restaurant. Both of his children answered with, "Yes ma'am and no ma'am, yes sir and no sir."

Piper came to the restaurant about 30 minutes late because her three-year-old was having a massive tantrum, as she explained to Darnell. Her five-year-old was very quiet, but a very picky eater, and when the waiter brought his chicken fingers, fries, and carrots, he threw his carrots on the floor. Piper's boys were out of control, yelling profusely, and hitting their mom when they couldn't have their way. Darnell's military background wanted to kick in so badly. He wanted to grab the boys and give them a little bit of *act right,* but he knew that would be inappropriate.

Darnell had very sweet children, even in their younger years, he and his ex-wife Brandi communicated their expectations to their children. Piper was a single parent and never had the luxury of them having their dad. Her husband passed away in a car accident when they were toddlers. She was thankful that her parents often drove down to get the boys and give her a break. Piper's boys were very spoiled and totally out of control, especially with her being a daycare owner. They never followed the rules like the other daycare children. At the restaurant, customers watched her boys as they wrestled at the table, picked in their noses, spoke very loudly, whined, and constantly talked back to their mom.

Darnell asked the boys to calm down, but they just stared at him. His children were so embarrassed, they were truly ready to go. Darnell decided that the night should end. He really liked Piper and was so happy that they had rekindled their friendship. It was like old times again, but he was so disappointed in how disrespectful her boys were to her and each other. Darnell grew up in Memphis, Tennessee with strict parents, that had a military background, and disrespect was never tolerated.

Piper was from Kansas City, Kansas and later moved to Memphis. In her eyes, raising your voice was considered a form of abuse. Darnell was fuming inside while at the restaurant but didn't want to react to keep the peace and friendship with Piper. Throughout the night, Piper kept making hints that she wanted something serious with Darnell. He was prepared to eventually ask Piper to become his steady girlfriend, but after the fiasco with her boys, he is considering having a change of heart. Could disrespectful children be a deal breaker for Darnell? When love comes knocking, will he answer?

In relationships, opposites do attract. Everyone may come from different backgrounds and totally different upbringings, but you must decide what works best for you and your family. If you feel strongly about making the relationship work, maybe you can both be fair and take some advice from each other. A disrespectful child should never be tolerated, it may be beneficial to take some advice from Darnell on discipline and maybe Darnell could learn some things from Piper on having fun and not always being uptight. However, no child should ever raise their hands to their parent, no matter their age.

Piper has been allowing this behavior for years and never corrected it because she is sad that the boys no longer have their dad. This is still no excuse for them to disrespect their mom. She must be open to positive criticism when it comes to her children. Darnell has been in her shoes with rearing his own children and from the looks of it, it seems that his method works. Her boys act out in public places because she allows it in private places. Piper must put her foot down before it gets totally out of control. At the daycare, they must understand that they must follow the rules too. What happens when they start Kindergarten? They won't be allowed to do what they want to do, there are rules to follow everywhere.

Keep in mind this transformation won't happen overnight because it has been allowed since they were toddlers. Darnell seemed to really be getting close with Piper and she feels the same way. She should be careful though; her disrespectful boys may be the deal breaker and he end the relationship because she won't allow him to be a father figure in their lives. Piper should be open to discipline her children and communicate to them that their previous behavior will no longer be tolerated.

Discipline is good for all children, it empowers structure, self-control, makes you feel good, and encourages them to manage their feelings and behaviors. Overall, it lays a great foundation for children to be focused, teaches responsibility, they have a positive outlook on life, they are better students, and lifelong learners. Her boys are still very young, occasionally reward them with their favorite snacks, stickers, and special play dates for good behavior. Use this as a teachable moment for the boys to follow. Once their behavior is under control, Darnell, Piper, and everyone else will be happier.

Chapter 13

Keep the Spark Alive

Remember your marriage is not the wedding. After the wedding and reception is over and you are off to your paradise of love, your honeymooning days in most marriages have a shelf life, but it doesn't have to be over. Love is just not enough. You can continue to have those butterfly feelings of excitement and anticipation that you had when you first started dating. Continue to bless your marriage with love and laughter. "Above all, love each other deeply, because love covers over a multitude of sins." **1 Peter 4:8.**

When you have discussions, be respectful and truthful. Learn to manage your emotions, just because you are in a relationship, it doesn't mean that you will agree on everything. Tempers should not flare up because he or she has their own opinion about a specific topic. If you are wrong, don't be so pig headed that you can't admit it, apologize, and move on. Be respectful of each other's differences and learn to forgive. A husband doesn't have to be perfect to make his significant other happy, just show love and compassion like you did when you first started dating. Your wife deserves to be treated like a queen. Go on date nights, roll play, spend quality time together, turn the music on and dance the night away. Figure out what your spouse likes to do and do that! Be intentional. You asked God to send you a good man, head of household, a provider. When will you allow your husband to lead and wear the pants? Don't let your independence cause division in the marriage and the two of you aren't able to work together and be on one accord.

Learn to appreciate the small things. Remember the extra steps you took to please your mate at the beginning, you groomed yourself, dressed to impress, gave compliments, exercised, gave her love and affection, communicated until the sun came up, showered her with occasional just because gifts and date nights. What happened to that guy? Look the part, your appearance means everything. Remember when you kept your hair and nails done, watched what you ate to keep a nice figure, you listened more and talked less, dressed sexy occasionally, showed love and kindness, had great conversations, didn't nag because things aren't going your way, drove him crazy with those stiletto heels, pleased him the way he like you to. What happened to that lady?

Although life gets complicated and children will change the marriage, you still must continue to put effort towards keeping each other interested. Stop using your children as an excuse to not be intimate with your spouse. Children want to see Mama and Daddy happy and in love. Everything doesn't have to be a routine. Be adventurous and have fun together. Yes, things will change, but it doesn't mean you can't continue to be fun and exciting. Sometimes maintaining silence may be the best remedy for the relationship. You don't always have to have the last word, learn to agree to disagree. As my Mama would always say, "every situation doesn't require an argument." You should distinguish between the battles you want to fight. Stay prayerful, because the enemy will attempt to come between your marriages to knock you off course. "Therefore, what God has joined together, let no one separate." **Mark 10:9**.

Don't take each other for granted and have a prideful heart, because that's not what people in love do. Always use words of kindness. Words are powerful and in the heat of an argument, you may just say things that you can't take back. Learn to pray and lean on God. You will forgive but never forget what was said. Stop having a bad day at the office and coming home taking it out on your mate. Your office problems should be left at your office door. Have a 20-minute rule to talk about work problems and then move on to better and happier topics.

Your relationship should involve the two of you, everyone doesn't have to be part of your decision making. Always maintain self-discipline within your marriage, and don't allow any bad habits or outside influences like drugs, alcohol, work, or people to interfere with your union. Know that you are not each other's enemy, you should be best friends, teammates, lifelong partners, ride or die for each other. Work out differences between both of you and remember to stop telling everyone your problems. When you have forgiven him or her, your family and friends still may continue to hold grudges.

Keep the passion and intimacy alive and well. I love when I'm cooking in the kitchen and my husband kisses me from behind on the back of my neck or grab me by my waist for a hug. This turns up the heat of passion in the kitchen. Intimacy doesn't always have to be in the bedroom, your children should see the love shared by their parents. Any flirtatious gesture, quick kiss or hug shown is a great way to teach your children how to love and be loved.

When my husband calls my name very aggressively from upstairs, and when I come running, he tells me oh, I just wanted to say that "I love you," it makes me feel special, like I'm the luckiest girl alive. He makes my toes curl when he kisses me along the small of my back. When we get our alone time, and the intimacy is at its highest peak, we can't get enough of each other, afterwards deciding to cuddle, watch a romantic movie, share stories, or listen to music.

DeMorris loves to compliment me about my sweet natural body odor and hair. It is the small things that get him aroused. I like it when he glimpses me in amazement that God blessed us with each other. We don't have a perfect marriage, and don't always see eye to eye, but we are truly blessed to have one another. My husband is my love beast, and after 18 years of togetherness, we knew we were meant to be together, because God was in the midst of it all. He loved me beyond my looks and physic, he makes love to my intellect, character, body, and purpose. "The husband should fulfill his marital duty to his wife, and likewise the wife to her husband." **1 Corinthians 7:3.**

We love each other's company, our best dreams were dreamed together, and some of our best laughs were laughed together, because we are companions. Ask yourself what can I do to make my partner happier? Play, have pillow talk, give that man or woman some *Ooh La La* loving and release the tension and stress that life brings. Spend quality time, take a road trip, enjoy a hobby, write love messages, hang around other loving couples, go dancing, and enjoy a picnic in the park. Learn to be open-minded and think outside of the box. Keep it spicy! It is ok to do something different, if you try it, you just might like it.

Remember love is not a feeling, it is an action and a choice. Have fun and don't stop being spontaneous because you are getting older. When the children are grown and gone, you must keep the love alive. Your partner deserves your unconditional friendship and love. No one knows the day nor the hour, enjoy your life while you can. Go above and beyond to keep a smile on your partners face. To have a happy marriage, the both of you have to want it bad enough to make it work. Be passionate. You deserve to enjoy a life of goodness. I pray that your beautiful union keeps the spark and continue to be showered with love and happiness from this moment throughout eternity. Continue to grow wiser, stronger, and better together in Christ.

Zoe met Kingston at sixteen living in the same neighborhood. It started off as mere puppy love but quickly grew into a serious romance. Kingston was a quarterback on the high school football team and Zoe was the captain of her cheerleading squad. The two of them were inseparable. Everybody knows Kingston will do well and make a lifelong career in football, because he has been playing and coached by the best coaches in the league since he was 7. As the relationship progress, Zoe's interest for cheer was no longer her top priority. She started focusing on making her boyfriend stand out amongst the scouts. Zoe was constantly researching colleges and football stats of other players to make sure her boyfriend will be a first round pick.

Kingston was very attractive and was often getting the attention from other girls at school. He denied his attraction for any of them, always telling Zoe that she was the apple of his eye. As his schedule was getting busier and busier their quality time begun to diminish. Zoe stepped down from being captain of the cheerleading squad and started working a part-time job to take her mind from the loneliness she was dealing with. After working there for about six months, she decided to quit and focus on her boyfriend's dreams. Zoe's mom, Shanice was a single mother and wondered what was happening to her daughter's excitement about her life. After her mom and dad got a divorce, Zoe started to regret cheering, fear that if her attention was focused on her passion, it would run Kingston away.

Shanice was a registered nurse and worked very long hours. Her schedule was very unpredictable, and Zoe blames her mom's career for ending their marriage. Shanice stayed on Zoe about applying to colleges, but she didn't want to jeopardize losing the relationship she had with Kingston. She pretended to fill out college applications to satisfy her mom's desire for her to attend college, but never completed any of them. Kingston wanted Zoe to be happy and pursue the college of her choice.

Zoe always had a desire to become a pediatrician. She loved children and was always interested in working in the medical field like her mom, but she continued to feel that her mom's career was the reason why her dad left. It is graduation day and Kingston had gotten academic and athletic scholarships from four different universities. His parents were elated with his hard work and determination to succeed.

Kingston's mom and dad had growing concerns about the relationship between him and Zoe because of her lack of enthusiasm to pursue college or a career. Anna, Kingston's mom decided to have a sit-down talk with Zoe as she saw her to be a potential daughter-in-law. Zoe told her that she would look for a part-time job and apply to the community college in the area. She started hanging with the wrong crowd and didn't apply for anything as she had promised. Zoe was insecure and decided to propose to Kingston to mark her territory. She loved him and was so afraid that he would lose interest in her once he becomes well known at the University. When love comes knocking, will he answer?

Kingston felt that Zoe was trying to pressure him into marriage, something he wasn't ready for. She began flirting with other guys to make him jealous. Kingston decided to end what was left of the relationship. Love shouldn't be a game. Kingston truly loved Zoe but refused to entertain the games she was playing for his attention. Although Kingston parents' liked Zoe, they were happy about the decision he had made to break up with her, because they knew he didn't have time for any distractions. They wanted to make sure he didn't lose his scholarships. Kingston always thought about Zoe, he hated the fact that she focused more on his dreams than her own. The breakup made Zoe think about her career goals and without hesitation she enrolled at the local University, about an hour from Kingston.

Many months had passed, and Zoe reached out to Kingston. He was truly happy to hear from her again, and even happier to find out that she was back in school. Kingston explained to Zoe that he didn't want to break up but wanted her to focus on her dreams. He assured her that she had his heart no matter how near or far they were from one another. Kingston shocked Zoe by telling her that he loved her. Zoe mentioned to Kingston that she had loved him for years but was afraid to tell him. She feared that her feelings wouldn't be reciprocated. Zoe also told him that she felt if she focused on her goals, eventually the love would be lost, and he may go to college and meet someone else. She didn't want to jeopardize their relationship because she was thinking of her own ambitions.

Kingston was shocked that Zoe thought so little of making herself a priority. He told her that she had to exude self-love before she could open her heart to be loved. He quickly put things in perspective for Zoe. He stated. "When I decide to settle down with my queen, I would like her to pursue her dreams, for us to build our empire together. I am not a selfish man, if God blesses me with gifts and talents, I should be receptive to honor and respect what gifts and talents God blesses upon my wife. The more knowledge and education we receive collectively, the better we are prepared for our future." Zoe didn't realize Kingston had even thought about a future with her, although they had been a couple off and on since their freshman year of high school.

Years had passed and Kingston and Zoe were becoming very serious. Graduation was upon them. Kingston wanted to make sure Zoe knew how much he loved her. He showed up with a dozen yellow roses, her favorite color, unannounced at the clinic where Zoe was doing her internship. She was called to the lobby on the intercom. Several of her co-workers started to gather in the lobby when they saw a shiny pear-shaped 4 carat diamond ring gleaming from a distance. They were in their senior year, getting ready to graduate from college and Kingston had gotten a few offers to play for the NFL. Zoe came downstairs smiling from ear to ear. Her boss had been acting suspicious all day and she later found out that he was part of the surprise.

Kingston got on one knee confessing his love to Zoe in front of the pediatric unit. He had gone weeks before and privately asked Zoe's dad for her hand in marriage and was happy to receive his and her mom's blessings. Not only did Kingston surprise her with the perfect marriage proposal, but also an offer to play football with the Seattle Seahawks, her favorite football team. Zoe asked her boss before she gave Kingston an answer if he would write her a letter of recommendation for an internship in Seattle. Her boss agreed. Zoe screamed, "YES!" She was so happy to spend the rest of her life with someone that truly cared about both of their successes. Love came knocking very unexpectedly

Chapter 14

Un-Neighborly Love

Coming home from picking the children up from school, Eva was greeted with luggage from her new neighbors sitting in her driveway. As she is inconvenienced, they slowly moved them. She gives a wave hello, but they are not looking in her direction. Bad vibes. The family is quite different than the rest of the neighborhood families. They seem to love the outdoors, and were often seen gathering outside, playing football in the street and baseball in the front yard. When the ball doesn't go inside the net, it hits Eva's garage door. Eva's oldest daughter is allergic to cats, and every morning when she opened the front door to walk to the bus stop, she had to jump over the neighbor's cat, who seemed to love the rug by their front door. When Eva looked outside the kitchen window, her children's trampoline had several holes torn in it from the neighbor's cat, who has lost his way back home again.

The Grandma of the new neighbors comes to visit her daughter often, and doesn't show herself friendly, always having a mean look on her face. *Exactly what I am thinking.* This is not a good way to be welcomed to the neighborhood. The husband was a football coach and never seemed to be at home, and the mom, well, she is a stay-at-home Mom, but you often see her young children keeping themselves outside, or at other neighbor's homes. Eva decided to walk to the neighborhood park, and on her way, she stopped to say hello to her new neighbor. Her neighbor introduced herself as Jillian, and confided in her that she was always alone, because her husband was never at home. Eva immediately knew that there was a lot of friction going on with this relationship.

Sadly, weeks passed by, and Eva never saw the neighbor's husband, but when he was at home, she witnessed verbal confrontations right in the front yard, around the children. Jillian, the wife goes on a trip and Eva sees the husband's constant infidelity within the marriage. He was seen bringing over the mothers of the boys he was coaching in football, with their small children around. It wasn't a good look, total disrespect of the marriage and the entire family. He doesn't seem to care about his marriage anymore, because he was so carefree with his adultery.

One day as Eva was closing her window blinds, she noticed that Jillian was talking privately in her car on the side of her house, like she was sneaking with someone else. It was very unpleasing to see two adults act in this manner with children involved. There was a lot of bad vibes with this family. Things Eva would like to complain about, like the cat, or the Grandma constantly parking right in front of her house, or the young boy throwing balls in her front yard, she decided not to because they seem to already have a lot of problems. People in the neighborhood started shying away from the daughter of the new neighbors because there were rumors that she had very sticky fingers and lies a lot.

Eva had a busy life. It was very unfortunate that she witnessed these disturbing behaviors from the new neighbors in a matter of a few months. A year later, while Eva and her family were packing up their truck to go on vacation, a moving truck was backing up to the neighbor's house, but they were only taking the wife, children, and the grandma's things. Eva and her family sadly witnessed a family break up right before their eyes, and the look in the children's eyes were heartbreaking. The Dad was the only one left in the house and immediately had many women visiting the home. Jillian was seen driving by occasionally, monitoring his whereabouts. The husband quickly decided to move on with his life and didn't seem to have a care in the world about losing a wife and three children.

The neighbor's seven-year-old daughter Victoria wasn't happy to start a new school but was excited to meet new friends. They only moved about thirty minutes away and was happy to see their dad when he came to visit. Victoria loved her new teacher and would often talk about her, it was a breath of fresh air for her to attend school, because her mom and dad truly disliked each other. Later Eva's husband found out that the neighbors were high school sweethearts but because of the ups and downs of life they had forgotten how to love one another. They couldn't stand being in the same room together, the break-up was bound to happen; it was only a matter of time.

Eva's girlfriend Abigail called to tell her that she had met a new guy. She doesn't go into many details but convinced her that he was her prince charming sent from God. Abigail was a second-grade teacher and usually has a good judgement of character when it comes to men. It has been a long time since she has been in a relationship, and she seems very happy. Abigail told Eva about a new student she has that acts very peculiar. She feels that the little girl was going through something personal at home but because she was new, she doesn't want to ask her any questions.

A year later, Eva finally gets to meet her girlfriend's boyfriend and she was so shocked and totally speechless. It was her neighbor, the cheater, adulterer, homewrecker, disrespectful husband that lived next door to her. Eva cannot believe that her girlfriend, who always had high standards has fallen for this sorry excuse of a man. Supposedly, he never brought her to his house because his ex-wife damaged the home inside before she left. Eva knew that his wife wasn't squeaky clean, and it takes two, but she saw Abigail's new boyfriend's unethical ways.

When Eva met Abigail's new boyfriend, Jonathan, she didn't say much, she stayed cordial, but felt very uncomfortable. Later, Eva called and told Abigail that her new boyfriend was her neighbor. Eva constantly tried to convince her girlfriend that he cannot be trusted. Abigail told Eva that Jonathan and his wife had gotten a divorce months ago and he was very active in his children's lives. Abigail shares with Eva that her new student is his seven-year-old daughter Victoria. She tells her that he regrets what happened with his marriage but was ready to move forward and wants to take their relationship to the next level. When love comes knocking, will her friend Abigail answer?

Eva loves her girlfriend Abigail and only wants the best for her. As her friend, you can share with her what you have observed, but ultimately it will be her decision. Your neighbor has plenty of baggage, and the way he has treated his wife, you are afraid that your friend may be his next victim. Make sure she is fully aware of what she is getting herself into. Not only will he have to pay child support, but alimony will come at a high price because they were married for over 10 years.

No couple gets married to get a divorce, but you know many families deal with this daily. The pandemic has caused a lot of couples to make the decision to go their separate ways. When there is confusion in the home, and your priority is not God, marriage, and family, you are setting yourself up for a failed relationship. Don't be surprised if the children start to act out for attention. Ask your girlfriend Abigail to consider the pros and cons of this relationship. Pay attention to his actions not words. She doesn't have children and will immediately go from zero children to three children with the youngest being two. Take your time and don't be too anxious in your opinions to your girlfriend. Listen well and speak the facts and hopefully after you have shared this information with her, the decision she makes, will be the best one for her.

Chapter 15

Pandemic Love

The world has become tainted with an infectious virus that has killed over 900,000 people in the United States. Michelle is so happy that very few of her family have suffered with positive cases, however, everyone hasn't been so lucky. Michelle is a 35-year-old artist, happy and loving her single life, but ready to find a new love. Her past relationships have made her really mistrust men, but after talking with her therapist, she tries to keep an open mind. She opened her own art gallery and hired some amazing staff to help her with her business. She hasn't dated in two years, and constantly has flashbacks of what she went through with her ex.

Michelle's ex-boyfriend Wendell was a personal trainer and used his training skills to solicit women. They met in college and both loved health and fitness. They both worked out at the gym every day together and knew their love would last forever. She trusted him, and although occasionally she was suspicious of his behavior, she gave him the benefit of the doubt. Michelle and Wendell dated for three years and was ready to take their relationship to the next level. She was the happiest girl alive when he proposed to her on Christmas 2018, but sadly, her new beginning turned into an abrupt ending in a matter of two months.

Michelle received flowers on Valentine's Day from Wendell or so she thought. As she read the card, she found out that it was from another personal trainer by the name of Isaac that worked at the same gym as her fiancé. *Why would he be sending her flowers?* The card explained to Michelle how she was a beautiful, loving, and caring person that deserved to be treated as such. It described her as being a flower, blossoming into something new and improved, letting go of old buds and leaves and growing some new ones.

After reading the riddles, Isaac, the personal trainer confessed that he had recently discovered that he and Michelle's fiancé Wendell were dating the same client, and now she is pregnant for Wendell. Michelle started to get emotional while reading the note. Isaac was positively sure that it wasn't his baby because he always wore protection. He didn't realize that she was playing both of them until he saw a text message appear on Portia's phone from Wendell. Isaac told Michelle that he confronted his client Portia and her fiancé Wendell, but it grew into an altercation, and he was forced by his boss to transfer to another gym.

Michelle felt her life was over, they had just closed on their brand-new home, bought cars together, were truly ready to start a brand-new life together. "Why would he do this to me?" Michelle asked. She had always been so loving and faithful to him. Michelle immediately confronted Wendell and there was so much tension they called off the engagement. He denied his wrongdoings for months, but the pieces to the puzzles started to all come together. After Michelle confronted his mistress Portia, she admitted to being his client for over a year and mentioned the personal attention she had been getting from Wendell after work hours.

She told Michelle that he had only mentioned having a girlfriend but not a fiancé, and his actions to her didn't indicate that he was in a serious relationship. After a lot of back and forth, Wendell ended up being the father of his client Portia's baby. Michelle moved out of the house and started renting at a nearby apartment. She felt that her life had been snatched away in a blink of an eye. What was more devastating, a few months later, Michelle found out that Wendell and Portia got married, and stayed in the house that he and Michelle had closed on. In Michelle's eyes, Portia stole her life away from her, and therapy was definitely needed.

The healing process was very lengthy, Michelle truly cried a river. Three years of her life she felt had been wasted. She put so much time and attention into their relationship. It took her a while, but after getting a closer relationship with God and having her family's support, she forgave Wendell and since then have moved on with her life. She consulted with her lawyer about removing her name from the assets that they had purchased together. It was the hardest thing to ever go through.

Their love was supposed to be forever. They talked about growing old together, raising their children and enjoying visits from their grandchildren one day. That relationship helped Michelle to have discernment in others, strength, and understanding in knowing what to look for in a potential mate. There were many red flags that she saw in Wendell when they first started dating that she chose to ignore. She was very thankful that God revealed his infidelity to her then and not years down the road.

After the breakup, Michelle decided that with her free time on the weekends she would join the Army National Guard. A few months had passed, and she was adjusting to her single life again. She had always loved to serve her community and her country. The National Guard allowed her to meet new people often responding to domestic emergencies, overseas combat missions, counterdrug efforts, reconstruction missions, and more. Michelle met a guy named Mark that had been placed in her vaccination squad. He was super funny, cool, and for some reason they were always placed in the same area to perform the vaccinations. At first, Michelle was skeptical to have a friendship with someone so soon, but she enjoyed having someone to talk to.

Her and Mark had gotten close over the past few months, they had so much in common, it's like their conversations were effortless. He sent a note to her asking her if she would be his girlfriend, with a "yes" or "no" box for her to check. It was the cutest gesture and without hesitation she checked "yes!" Their day was spent sharing funny stories of the different people they met. They were in disbelief that so many adults were horrified of needles. After work, they often spent hours on the phone, enjoyed happy hour, the park, or their favorite, her art gallery. What was so amazing, Mark was a professional photographer, and had many prestigious clients in the community. His work was very well known in the city. With her artistic skills of painting and drawing and his photography in capturing life's precious moments, they made the perfect team.

Although she was afraid to love again, she was open to give love another chance. Mark expressed to her how he felt that they had something special. He hadn't ever been married and didn't have any children, but often thought about settling down with someone special. She felt that Mark was very genuine but because of what she had gone through, it made her weary of the unknown.

Mark asked Michelle to be in an inclusive relationship with him after dating for nearly 6 months. He started talking about having a future with Michelle. He was approaching his mid-thirties and told her that he was ready for something serious. Michelle was having strong feelings for Mark too but started experiencing major hesitation because of the hurt she had endured with her ex-fiancé Wendell. Her life seemed very exciting and was getting very interesting until the unthinkable happened, Mark was transferred to another location to perform the vaccinations. When love comes knocking, will she answer?

Although it is very hard, you can't compare every guy you meet with your ex. Never make your present guy suffer from the mistakes made by your former guy. If you continue to dwell on the past, you may miss out on the blessing that God has especially for you. You and Mark seem to have laid a solid foundation that could continue with time and effort. He seems very open about his feelings he has for you. You have seen him every day for the last few months, but it doesn't mean that the relationship won't continue to prosper with him working at another location. Keep the communication open, take your time, stay prayerful and see where this potential love may take you.

Cheri and Drew met online during the pandemic, they are recent college graduates and were getting ready to attend graduate school in the fall. Cheri has spoken very highly of her internet hunk to her family, but all the communication has been online. She was anticipating the city opening back up so they will be able to meet in person. The conversations between the two has always been so wonderful and engaging. Drew calls Cheri throughout the day to tell her that he is thinking of her.

Cheri is beginning to fall in love with Drew but feels once she tells him about her decision to abstain from having sex until she gets married, he may become uninterested in her. Cheri's friends tease her quite often about not enjoying being single and hints that she is missing out on the spice of life because of her decision to practice abstinence.

Cheri is very strong in her faith, and although she is being teased, she stands firm in her beliefs. The spread of positive coronavirus cases is decreasing, and restaurants are beginning to open at full capacity. Drew asked Cheri out on a date to go to the local pub. This will be the first time that they meet in person. When he arrived, she was happy that he looked exactly like his profile picture, and both seemed pleased with each other.

After two months of dating, the relationship seemed to get stronger and stronger, and after the third date, Drew decided to go in for a kiss. Cheri enjoyed the kiss until things began to get very heated, and she decided to pump the brakes on the intimacy. She mentioned to Drew of her decision to wait until she was married before engaging in any sexual activity. Out of nowhere, Drew pulls out a beautiful shiny diamond ring and proposes to Cheri. She was speechless because this was never something she thought would happen so soon. Neither Cheri nor Drew have met each other's families. When love comes knocking, will she answer?

Let's start by looking at the timing of the relationship. First, you've only known Drew face to face for one month, because you spent one month chatting online, and this doesn't necessarily count as dating yet. Your family or friends haven't met him. Although you may want to keep some things personal, it is very important to get the opinions of the ones you trust before making any type of life-changing decisions.

How well do you know each other besides what you entered on your online profile? Sometimes putting specifics about yourself may eventually make you a target. Did you do a background check on Drew? Do you two share mutual friends? Where is he from? Is Drew his real name? These are the types of questions you may want to consider before meeting someone face to face. It is wise to take a friend or family member when you first meet a stranger.

This is a crazy world we live in, and you can't trust everyone you meet. After doing thorough research, Cheri finds out that Drew was a professional prankster that targets young, vulnerable, college students that is desperate to find love. He thrives on leading women on and getting their hopes up high. He takes advantage of them to get what he wants, dumps them, and moves on to his next victim. This was something that he and his buddies created while bored during the start of the pandemic. Like many other women, Cheri messed up by including too much information on her profile about practicing abstinence. Seeing this gave Drew an adrenalin rush to pursue her as a victim.

Drew had no intentions of marrying Cheri; it was one of his pranks to get what he wants from her. Kudos!! Cheri stood her ground and did not give in. Thankfully, her date with Drew didn't tragically end, and she was able to return home safely. True friends won't ever pressure you into doing something that you are not ready to do. Cheri learned from her mistakes, she immediately changed her number and decided that online dating took more work than she was willing to invest in. She started focusing on continuing her path of abstinence and getting ready for graduate school.

Cheri hasn't fully given up on online dating but plans to re-visit it later. Whether you decide to date the traditional way or online, do a background check, and always meet in public places. You must get to know as much information as you can, be open-minded, don't have any high expectations, avoid talking about sex, enjoy the conversation, but be cautious. Remember, you don't know this person, so if things don't work out, it is ok. If you enjoyed the date and would like to meet again, express that idea. This way it will help both of you understand each other's opinions about the date and help eliminate any confusion in the future. Never feel bad about making the right choices for the life you want to live.

Chapter 16

A Different Kind of Love

Xavier had a rough week at work, everything that could have gone wrong went there and then some. He has been working for the FBI for many years. He started out working as a police officer and later got a job offer to work with the Federal Bureau of Investigation. His weekends were always spent hanging out at the sports bar eating chicken wings and drinking beer, playing pool, while watching sports with the fellas.

Although, he looked forward to a night out with the boys, he was ready for a steady relationship with a special lady. Xavier's last relationship ended with his girlfriend Sierra of two years finding out that she was pregnant, but it wasn't his baby, it was for one of his fraternity brothers. Xavier's life had been torn to pieces, and it took a long time for him to have forgiveness in his heart for her or him. He felt truly betrayed by his fraternity brother and his girlfriend.

Xavier was often teased by his friends because he is a private investigator, but he got played by his own unattractive girlfriend. It wasn't that Sierra was ugly, but she didn't put forth a lot of effort in her appearance. She wasn't as spontaneous as he would have liked because she worked a lot of long hours. Sierra lived with her parents; she was a pharmaceutical manager. He always decided that his next relationship, she would have killer beauty and brains, she would be an independent woman with her own house and car.

Xavier was so upset about the affair that his girlfriend had, because he persuaded her to hire his fraternity brother, who had just graduated from pharmacy school. Although Xavier had started getting bored in the relationship with her, he felt that they were destined to be together, because they had known each other since elementary school. He knew that his queen was out there somewhere, it was only a matter of time before they find each other. On his way home from work, Xavier stopped by Home Expo to pick up some supplies because he had just bought a bungalow that was a fixer upper.

Xavier owned a lot of rental properties in the area that he would fix up and lease to his tenants. One day as he was visiting one of his properties, a gorgeous woman walked out of the house next door that had been on the market for sale. He waved hello to her, and she asked, "Are you, my neighbor?" Xavier told her that he owned a few of the properties in the neighborhood and he was checking to make sure they had been landscaped. She introduced herself, "My name is Brooklyn, and I am a first-time homeowner of this property." "Wow!! Congratulations!!" Xavier said. In his mind, he thought, *she's beautiful and a homeowner, he truly felt that God had answered his prayers.*

He stayed away for a while because Brooklyn had just closed on her home and hadn't started to move in yet. He also wanted to make sure she didn't think he was stalking her, but he really wanted to get to know her better. Xavier noticed that she didn't have a ring on her finger and was hoping that she wasn't in a relationship. A couple of months had passed, and he saw her checking her mail again when he decided to make his move. He asked her if she was seeing anyone and immediately, she said no. Brooklyn accepted his invitation to go out on a date. After three months, Xavier and Brooklyn were an official couple. He started telling his friends about her, even some of his family members. Brooklyn was the principal of the nearby elementary school; she hadn't been married and didn't have any children. Xavier admired her because she was perfect in every way, he couldn't believe that she was single. Xavier invited her over and surprised her with a romantic dinner for two in his backyard with a violinist and a personal sous chef.

Brooklyn was very grateful for his thoughtfulness. It had been 6 months after she had moved into her new house, and she decided to invite Xavier over to her place for a nightcap. He was so excited because he wanted to visit her new home for a while but wanted to take things slow and be respectful of her. She left his house before him, and he decided to pack a small bag just in case he would be spending the night. Xavier was on Cloud 9! He felt like he had struck the jackpot with this relationship, until he arrived at her house. Xavier had really started to have strong feelings for her. Brooklyn greeted him at the door looking nice and refreshed as she had taken a shower and put on her pajamas.

When the door opened, Xavier was in total shock! He could hardly get inside the house. Clutter was everywhere! Her house was a total mess inside. It looked like she never threw away anything but collected everything! In every nook and cranny there was mail, newspapers, books, boxes, containers, pictures, paper, food, clothes, it wasn't even enough space for Xavier to sit down on the sofa. Brooklyn is an extreme hoarder! She acted normal and was happy to take Xavier on a tour of her three-bedroom home. Clothes and clutter were all over the place. Principal Brooklyn desperately needed to take a class in organizational skills.

Xavier thought that the house was beautiful, but every room was filled with nonsense. He went to the bathroom and could hardly see the bathtub because it seemed to be used as storage space for her knick-knacks. *How can someone be a professional administrator, look so good on the outside and be so filthy?* Xavier thought. He was so shocked and truly disappointed. He could not believe that a woman with such brains and beauty could live like this. From the outside Brooklyn seemed so well and put together, but when he stepped inside her home.....oh my goodness! A couple of his guy friends called him the next day to see how the date went, and he had so much to tell them about his night that he began to stutter. Xavier was really considering introducing Brooklyn to his friends and family. Are filthy habits a deal breaker for Xavier? When love comes knocking, will he answer?

Xavier has been through a lot when it comes to relationships, but love is still out there somewhere. All relationships have problems but there is also a solution if you care to stick around. Sierra and your fraternity brother betrayed you for having a good heart and looking out for a friend by recommending employment through your girlfriend. They both took advantage of your love and kindness. You met Brooklyn and you thought she had it all together beauty and brains, independent woman with a promising career. Sadly, her lifestyle of being an excessive hoarder has truly changed the trajectory of where the relationship could have been headed.

All is not lost, because you haven't had a thorough conversation with Brooklyn to find out more about her and her unwelcoming hoarding. If you feel that there is hope for the two of you, be real with her and have a conversation without judgement. Consider peeling back the layers to see what is really going on.

Your conversation should start off something like this. Brooklyn, I see you have a lot of collectables. Can you tell me the history of some of them? In Brooklyn's mind, maybe she doesn't see it as being extreme and doesn't feel she has a problem. Do a little bit of probing to find out where this stemmed from. Does her mom, dad, Grandma, or any other family members have a hard time letting go of possessions? There may be deeper issues and opening the conversation may help you get to the root cause. No one is perfect and maybe you are the right person to get her the help that she may need. We all have some struggles that we are dealing with, some greater than others, but if you care for someone, running away from the problem is not the answer.

Hoarding is a disorder and sometimes it can be caused by someone losing a loved one and always holding on to the memory of that person by keeping their belongings. It can be a mental illness also related to a person having a stressful life that they had difficulty coping with such things as a divorce, losing possessions in a fire, or evictions.

If you see a possible future with Brooklyn, have effective communication about your feelings for her, ask questions, and discuss how her habit of hoarding may affect the relationship. You may have to seek professional help to make sure she has an advocate, because depending on how long this has been going on, it may not be an easy task and will require some professional assistance. Understand throwing things away may create distress and anxiety for your partner. You may be the only one that she trusts to help her get rid of the clutter and work on her cleanliness. Assure her that you want to help her without judgement, and don't let the mess create stress in the relationship.

Layla and London are identical twins from Sweet Home Alabama. They are well known in their community because they are both medical doctors. Layla specializes in pediatrics and London in obstetrics and gynecology. They are in their mid-thirties and have been longing for a forever love. Their parents passed away from cancer shortly after they graduated from medical school and their Uncle Theodis became their father figure. He has always been their favorite uncle because he was smart, funny, and was known in the family as the *Love Doctor*. His track record for setting up family members and the longevity of the marriages has been extraordinary.

Uncle Theodis is seventy-five and shined shoes back in the day for a local shoe store owner. All the locals knew him and would always recommend him to the out of towners. Mr. & Mrs. Corrigan, the shoe store owners never saw Theodis as the help, but part of their family. When they got older, they did a last will and testament and left the store, and 1 million dollars to Theodis and his wife Nadine. The store owners were never blessed with children, and their nieces and nephews weren't responsible enough to keep the store thriving. Theodis knew so many people in the community and beyond, it was very easy for him to run the store. Theodis played matchmaker with his customers, and some have even invited him to their weddings and special events.

Theodis would always suggest to his nieces to be unbiased when it comes to love. Although they have wonderful careers in the medical industry, he wanted them to understand that their mate may not be a Harvard graduate, but it doesn't mean he won't be successful. Theodis loved his nieces like they were his own, but felt they were a little bougie when it came to love. He had a high school buddy that had moved up north and had twin sons that lived only an hour away. He had known these boys since they were infants and admired how well they turned out as grown men. Uncle Theodis had been dwelling on the idea of telling his nieces about the guys for a while but felt God would eventually place someone in the girl's path, but they were always working.

Aunt Nadine suggested to invite the guys to the store's 50th Anniversary Celebration and that way they could meet the girls. The twins Bryce and Braxton were excited about the invitation to attend the celebration because they hadn't seen them in years but had no clue that they were playing match maker. When they arrived, Uncle Theodis asked them if they had a special lady. Both guys said, "No, but do you know anyone?" Uncle Theodis and Aunt Nadine chuckled. They were so happy that both were single, with no children and actively looking for a wife. The guys were business owners of a grave excavation service. You may be wondering what exactly does this mean. It is a ditch digging business. Both boys are college graduates but always loved getting their hands dirty. They have several large contracts with reputable funeral homes and well-known cemeteries across the United States. Their business is one of the top black-owned businesses in the industry, bringing in over three million dollars in revenue each year.

Uncle Theodis started telling the guys about his nieces and suggested if they asked what they did for a living, to just tell them they worked in the funeral business. Aunt Nadine didn't like that her husband was telling them to say that and suggested for them to be truthful in hopes that the girls won't be judgmental. The guys are very successful, and it is an honest and legitimate career. The day had arrived and Theodis was so excited about celebrating his stores 50th year celebration, but more excited that his nieces will finally meet his friends.

The girls had no clue what their uncle and aunt was up to. London arrived first and was immediately connected with Braxton. It was all laughter and smiles throughout the evening. Aunt Nadine called Layla to make sure she was coming, thankfully she was right around the corner, just delayed because of traffic. Bryce approached Layla as she entered the building, and they seem to really hit it off. The girls were always used to dating guys in the medical field, wearing lab coats, the preppy boy type that their uncle frowned upon. He wanted them to broaden their interest a little, to understand that there are successful guys that work blue collar jobs too.

The double daters seem to have truly enjoyed the celebration. They all thanked Uncle Theodis and Aunt Nadine for the invite and especially introducing them to their dates for the evening. When the girls asked Bryce and Braxton what they did for a living, they answered, "We are grave diggers!" When love comes knocking.....will the girls answer?

Months had passed by, and the girls never seem to mention Bryce and Braxton to their aunt and uncle. Uncle Theodis and Aunt Nadine didn't want to pry, but they really wanted to know the status of their relationships. Secretly, Bryce and Layla, and Braxton and London were still dating and enjoying each other's company. The girls took their uncles advice years ago about being open to love. They didn't judge the guys on their career path because they love what they do, they are very successful, and like the medical industry, business will be plentiful, always having a steady income.

Every other weekend the sets of twins would go on double dates. Christmas was approaching and the girls were ready to surprise their families by letting them know that their relationships had been going well. The guys and their parents arrived, and Aunt Nadine and Uncle Theodis was ready to enjoy their company for the holidays. London and Layla rode together and was about to surprise their family of the status of their relationship with Bryce and Braxton, but they didn't realize they were about to get the ultimate surprise. Bryce and Braxton had contacted Uncle Theodis weeks before Christmas to discuss visiting them for the holidays and asking him for permission to marry London and Layla. Both guys got on one knee after Christmas dinner and asked for London and Layla's hand in marriage. With tears in their eyes, both girls screamed "YES!" Not only did love come knocking, but the door was opened twice to a different kind of love filled with success.

Chapter 17

What Is Love?

"Love is patient, love is kind. It does not envy, it does not boast, it is not proud." **1 Corinthians 13:4.** Love is never glad about the injustices of life but rejoices whenever truth wins. If you love someone you will respect and be loyal to him or her. If he or she loves you, they will never put you in uncompromising situations. Love handles conflict constructively. Love is not selfish or jealous. Love heals, restores, repairs, bears all things, believes all things, hopes all things, and endures all things. **1 Corinthians 13:7** Love is cherishing your mate till death do you part. Love accepts imperfections. Love never fails, love prevails. Love is learning to chase your goals walking hand and hand. Love is waking up with a kiss of gratitude. It is appreciating the small things in life. Love is sharing and caring for one another. Love is flexibility, it is being open to new ideas and different ways of doing things. Love is loving yourself and knowing that you are enough.

Love is making sure you and your spouse are happy and healthy. It is an exchange of thoughtfulness and support. It is admitting that you are wrong and asking for forgiveness to make it right. Love is a constant work in progress. L is for the way we LIVE our lives through all our ups and downs. It is how we continue to have a lifelong LOVE and infatuation with each other, even as we get older. It is the way we make each other LAUGH, until we are about to burst. O is for the way we take OWNERSHIP in being great partners and providers, we are always OPEN to show our true selves. We are the OXYGEN to each other's tank; we show an OVERFLOW of love when we need it the most. V is for the everyday VALENTINE we are to each other, whether we agree to disagree. We are the VOICE of life when we're at our strongest and our weakest. E is for the EFFORT we have every day in being a better spouse and parent. The EXTRA love, kindness, respect, patience and understanding we give in our walk of life as one. Love is only a four-letter word until someone comes along and gives it meaning. We thank God for our love.

Dedication

I dedicate this book to anyone who has found true love, in search of love, or bitter from love, you are not alone. Finding true agape love can be hard, but you must allow the blessings that God has for you to manifest into what is meant for you. Whether you are in a relationship or not, learn to love yourself first and enjoy your life in the present, because tomorrow isn't promised. Life can be filled with obstacles, and you may have to experience a lot of heartaches and heartbreaks to know what you can endure. Through the storm and rain, joy will come in the morning. Patience is the key to receiving the full desires of your heart. Be open to love.

Acknowledgments

We are grateful for the love and blessings from God to be able to experience wonderful relationships.

SUSU Entertainment LLC is so thankful to have our family and friends participate in our couple's love project, to share their journey of love and words of wisdom with our readers about their marriages. What is the glue that holds everything together? What is the secret to their longevity? We pray that these love stories will inspire anyone that is getting ready to settle down and jump into a life of forever with the one they love.

Willie Earl and Beaster H. Lewis
Wedding Date: November 17, 1973

Willie Earl: We lived in the same neighborhood; our families knew each other. I had graduated from high school and really wanted to get to know Beaster better, however, her mom wouldn't allow her to have any company. Every time I saw her walking in the neighborhood, I use that opportunity to walk with her.

Beaster: My husband and my oldest brother Willie (Peter) are friends and classmates, but I was formally introduced to him by his younger sister, Katherine Lewis. Our friends and I were waiting for the school bell to ring and Kat said, "My brother Willie Earl likes somebody in this group." When I asked, "Who?" She said, "You!" I walked off saying, "I don't like that boy!" 48 years later, 2 beautiful daughters, Valanda and LaWanda, and four wonderful grandchildren, Neziah, Nylah, Nalin, and Bianca, I guess I'm still not liking that boy.

Words of Wisdom: "In all thy ways acknowledge him and he shall direct thy paths." Proverbs 3:6.

Darryl and Valanda Covington
Wedding Date: August 20, 2010

Our journey in finding love and staying in love started with our online profiles on an internet dating site. We listed our likes, dislikes, status, future aspirations and then waited for a true match. After the first email, it was clear that the words were right, but would the actions follow? We had long talks, a shared attraction, and the usual belly butterflies of a new romance.

We understood that we came to each other with strengths and weaknesses and we both vowed to love, enjoy, support, respect and basically be there for each other through everything. We are blessed to be married for 11 years and have a beautiful 8-year-old daughter, Bianca.

Words of Wisdom: To love is great. To be loved is wonderful, but to be loved by the person you love is everything. We are so happy we swiped right!

Demeetron and Nicole Burrell
Wedding Date: July 3, 2014

We were introduced to each other by a mutual friend that I worked with. Her husband served in the military with Demeetron. My husband was active duty for 11 years and has been in the U.S. Air Force Reserve for the past 7 years. I knew Demeetron was "The One," just by him genuinely being a nice guy. He always made time for me, even after he was tired from a trip and was on a different sleep schedule from military assignments. Most importantly, he was good to my daughter, he loved her, and she loved him. We have two beautiful children, ages 14 and 4.

Words of Wisdom: A strong, healthy relationship revolves around spending quality time together, making sure that he or she knows that they are a priority and just appreciating each other's presence. It's easy to lose sight of these things in our busy day to day lives, between kids and work, but making time for each other is a must to keep our relationship moving forward.

John and Betty L. Savage Boggan
Wedding Date: December 24, 1966

John and I were born and raised in Greenville, Alabama. We met picking cotton in the cotton field. John was a field worker, and I was a secretary, responsible for weighing the cotton and paying the workers off. Even though John was anticipating getting to the end of his row, he didn't realize until later that he would be picking more than just cotton. We have been married for 55 years and blessed with one daughter, five granddaughters, eight great-granddaughters, and a girl dog.

Words of Wisdom: David says, "The Lord is my shepherd, I shall not want." Remember whatever you do always put God first.

Patrick and Deborah Georges

Wedding Date: March 1, 1988

We met at a nightclub, his friends took him out and my friends did the same for me. I went straight from work, still wearing my name tag. Patrick asked me to dance, I didn't like him at first, but I accepted. The next day, he showed up at my job, and the rest is history. We are blessed with five children and eleven grandchildren.

Words of Wisdom: Marriage is the foundation of family, and family is the fundamental unit of society.

You can help the flowers blossom and grow by watering and paying close attention to them, or you can ignore the plant and let the roots dry out and die. We talk, not yell and we don't keep secrets from each other. We don't belittle one another because we always know that our partner has our back. Our marriage is like a palm tree, we bend and not break. A palm branch is a symbol of victory, triumph, peace, and eternal life.

Ralph and Hattie Covington
Wedding Date: June 30, 1959

Ralph and I are from New York and met while working at the hospital, I was a Nurse's Aide, and he was an Orderly. After a year of courtship, we were married. From our union, we were blessed with two biological children and 4 bonus children that we inherited, 12 grandchildren, 9 great-grandchildren, and 2 great-grandchildren on the way.

Words of Wisdom: After 62 years of marriage, we have benefited from these tips for a successful marriage. COMMUNICATION, talking and listening is very important; LAUGHTER, brings joy into your marriage; TOUCHING, reduces stress and pain; MONEY, budget and work together; SPEND TIME TOGETHER, grow together, not apart; LITTLE SURPRISES, are always good for your marriage; SHARING, household chores and rearing children is everyone's job; OFFERING ADVICE, sometimes you just need an ear and empathy; CHILDREN, you must always show that you are united in any decisions; GOD IN YOUR HOME, God's spiritual guidance is necessary in your home to smooth the way for a lasting happy marriage.

Allin and Betty Loveless Whittle
Wedding Date: June 3, 1973

We are Allin and Betty Loveless Whittle and we've been married for 48 years but together for 51 years. We have been blessed with 2 awesome children and 4 terrific grandkids. Our story began on Commerce Street in Greenville, Alabama. I rode on the back of my grandfather's truck while they did their Saturday shopping, and I would always see this boy, who never spoke to me, but always stared at me! A year later, we officially met in our math class at Alabama A & M University. We had similar interests in college, he pledged Phi Beta Sigma Fraternity, Inc., and I pledged the sister organization, my beloved Zeta Phi Beta Sorority, Inc. We started out with nothing and built a life together in our loving home with our family.

Words of Wisdom: I am not saying to do it our way, but you must work together, trust each other, it is give and take, and always put your faith in God. Who knows you may be the next Allin and Betty L. Whittle, 48 years strong!

Brian and Ahrei Pennington
Wedding Date: June 20, 2009

We are Brian and Ahrei Pennington. We have been married for 12 years and blessed with three beautiful children, 2 sons, ages 10, 9, and a daughter, 7. We met while partying at the club in Los Angeles, California, my hometown.

Words of Wisdom:

1- Always keep God first and pray together every day. Matthew 18:20

2- Go to pre-marital counseling before getting married. We went once a week for three months before getting married.

3- Never go to bed angry.

Henry & Frances Herbert
Wedding Date: February 23, 1974

We met in high school, my cousin, James Wilson introduced us to one another. We got married at a young age, so therefore we were in the learning process. We were blessed with two children, Desmond, and Deidre, and six grandchildren, Desiree, Kiarra, Kamari, Ayana, Elyse, and Khloe.

Words of wisdom:

Married couples should remember marriage is like gardening, you must keep working at it so it will thrive and survive on good and bad days. One of our favorite scriptures is 1 Peter 4:8. "And above all, love each other deeply, because love covers a multitude of sin."

Malcolm & Lashonda Fields
Wedding Date: November 22, 2000

We met in high school. He approached me. I honestly was not interested. He asked for my number, and I refused. He took it upon himself to look me up in the phone book and call me. Malcolm was persistent, friendly, and charming. He won me over, and the rest is history. We are blessed with three children, two girls and a boy.

My Words of Wisdom: Know why you are getting married in the first place. Know that it is a process, and that it takes time and energy to grow, nurture and maintain your relationship. Know that there is a difference between having a "successful wedding" and a "successful marriage." Lastly, make FORGIVENESS and patience big priorities in your relationship.

His Words of Wisdom: Put God's word first and foremost. Marriage is a union that should be unconditional. There will be "ups," and there will be "downs." However, what you value in your marriage, will determine how you respond to those "ups" and "downs." Let God's word be the foundation of your marriage. Let wisdom be the walls, and let LOVE be the roof.

Frank and Janet Lewis
Wedding Date: August 25, 1973

Frank and I met at his mother's house. His sister and I were members of the same church during that time. The blessings of God sealed the union, and four beautiful children were born and two grandchildren.

Words of Wisdom:

Prayers were the rails laid for a soul mate. Truth and honesty were the binding to unity and longevity for our marriage.

Anthony and Angela Williams
Wedding Date: April 5, 2003

Our fathers were childhood friends. We met as children when Anthony's family came down to Houston for a summer visit. Years later, we were reintroduced to one another as young adults at Anthony's brother's wedding. We became friends, kept in touch, and started dating about 2 years after we became friends.

We were married almost 7 years before we were blessed with our first child. We now have two sons, Anthony Jr., 11 and Andrew, 7.

Words of Wisdom: You must both make a conscious decision to be together through the good and bad times. Remember to never take one another for granted because tomorrow is not promised. During disagreements, always remain respectful, listen to one another and be slow to anger and quick to forgive. Most importantly, remain the best of friends.

Jimmy and Vonnie Lawson
Wedding Date: June 29, 1969

Jimmy and I met through a mutual friend. Courtship began and soon we indulged in our marriage journey. After two years of marriage, we became proud parents of our daughter, Yolanda. We were so happy to receive our bundle of joy. We have also been blessed with two wonderful grandsons, Trey, 20 and Jayden, 17.

Words of Wisdom:

Marriage is laughter, a cheerful heart is like good medicine; but a crushed spirit dries up the bones. (Proverbs 17:22) These last 52 years has been the biggest blessing other than life itself.

Marcus & Tonia Ellis
Wedding Date: July 3, 2011

Marcus and I have known each other since high school. We have three beautiful children.

Words of Wisdom:

Marriage is a living thing. It takes work, communication, nourishment, and love to survive. You must feed into your marriage, care for it, respect it and always remember why God put you together to form a union. As with life, marriage has ups and downs, but no matter what happens...at the end of the day ALWAYS be able to say, "I love you."

Nathaniel and Sadie Mahand
Wedding Date: June 21, 1969

We were childhood friends and neighbors. We got married and was later blessed with 5 children, 10 grandchildren, and 3 great-grandchildren. Our picture is from our 50th Anniversary/Renewal Ceremony.

Words of Wisdom: Nathaniel: First, in order to receive wisdom, you must have sound understanding. It's imperative to believe and know thy self. In regard to wisdom in marriage, it's about your daily walk with God's mighty hand guiding you. Establish what you're willing to hold on to.... that's love!!!

Sadie: Trust. With trust, you must believe and stay prayed up. God will help you in any situation you're going through. Proverbs 3: 5-6

Gregory and Crystal Smith
Wedding Date: March 2, 2002

Gregory's grandparents were my neighbors growing up. Gregory and I did not connect during our younger years, but after I moved away and came home to visit, we hung out in a group twice. When I returned home for Thanksgiving, he stopped by my parent's home with a white rose and expressed his interest to get to know me further. Five months later, we got married, and God blessed our union with three wonderful children, Caleb, Josiah, and Serenity.

Words of wisdom: Marriage is honorable and a gift from God, and you should always treat it in that manner. Remember that we do not innately know how to sustain this union, and if you try in your own strength and limited understanding, the chances are that you will not have long-term success. Since God is the creator of this union, look to Him first for instructions for marriage through the study of the scriptures, prayer, and godly counsel.

Steven and Joyce Buskey
Wedding Date: September 1, 1984

Steven and I have been friends for a very long time, we were high school classmates. We have no children, we like to say, we are each other's baby.

Words of Wisdom:

To have happiness is to never leave home or retire to bed angry, for your love will forever last. Amos 3:3 says, "Can two walk together except they be agreed?" Our glue is prayer, compromise and being on one accord!

Joe and Rosalinda Elias
Wedding Date: January 31, 2011

About 12 and a half years ago a sweet lady, my mother-in-law, introduced me to her son Joe at Lakewood Church in Houston, Texas. A year and three months later we were married. There is a 19-year age gap between Joe and me. In our blended family, we have 8 children, 14 grandchildren, 19 great-grandchildren, and 6 great-great grandchildren.

Words of Wisdom:

We both have experienced seasons of heartache and pain, but we can truly say that God gave us beauty for our ashes. "Make every effort to keep yourselves united in the Spirit binding yourselves together in peace." Ephesians 4:3

Sebbie and Lola Lewis
Wedding Date: September 28, 1968

We both met each other in high school. We got married and was blessed with one son and one granddaughter.

Words of Wisdom:

Remember both husband and wife have to be committed and have God as their priority in order for their marriage to grow.

Martin and Kelley Phillips
Wedding Date: October 18, 1996

We met as Civil Engineering students at The University of Alabama in Tuscaloosa, Alabama, where we both pledged the brother and sister organizations, Phi Beta Sigma Fraternity, Inc., and Zeta Phi Beta Sorority, Inc. We have 3 sons ages 22, 19, and 14.

Words of Wisdom:

Honest and authentic communication is the key to a successful marriage. Don't be scared to have the difficult conversations with your spouse. Tell each other how you feel. Be honest and vulnerable.

Robert and Ceola Bennett
Wedding Date: December 28, 1948

The World War II Veteran and his beautiful bride established their roots in the Mount Zion Community, in Greenville, Alabama, blessed with 6 children, 10 grandchildren, and 14 great grandchildren!

Robert was a mail carrier for the U. S. Postal Service until he retired. Ceola was a homemaker where she devoted her life to supporting her husband and raising their 6 children, which included one autistic daughter. The family also maintained and operated their own farm, raising livestock and crops across numerous acres.

Words of Wisdom: Mr. and Mrs. Bennett give their credits to a long and productive marriage by keeping God first and honoring their vows. 73 years of togetherness!

Tyrail and Demeetra Toney
Wedding Date: October 10, 2017

Tyrail and I met in 2016 at my 23rd birthday party, where I invited our mutual friend and he decided to come along, that's when he noticed me. We didn't talk much at the party, but later that week he reached out to me, and we went on our first date to the movies and Fuzzy's Tacos in Oklahoma. From there, we instantly connected and have been married for 4 years and blessed with our 4-year-old son, Tristan.

Words of Wisdom:

While being married, one thing we can say especially with both of us being in the United States Air Force, is to never stop dating and always communicate. There may be missed anniversaries and birthdays due to military assignments, but a good marriage can't be found, but can be made.

DeMorris and LaWanda Lewis Burrell
Wedding Date: December 17, 2005

Our journey of love began at work on June 6, 2003. DeMorris worked as a security officer in a Houston high rise building. He quickly learned that his new assigned location had more than just cameras to watch, as he secures the heart of LaWanda an HR Professional.

We have been happily married for 16 years and blessed with three beautiful children. We are business owners of SUSU Entertainment LLC, a book writing, audiobook narrations, and book publishing company. Our written and published works include: "Stand Up, Speak Up, Because Your Time's Up," "The Adventures of Captain Midnight," "I Need Thee," and "When Love Comes Knocking."

Words of Wisdom:

We believe that your life is what you make it, whether you are single or married, love yourself, stay connected to the Most High God, live in your purpose and choose happiness

Let's Connect

EMAIL

susuentertainmentllc@gmail.com

FACEBOOK

@authorlawandaburrell

INSTAGRAM

@wandavision2020

TWITTER

@LaWandaLewisBu2

LINKEDIN

linkedin.com/in/lawanda-lewis-burrell-58b80480

WEBSITE

www.susuentertainmentllc.com

About The Author

LaWanda Lewis Burrell is a faith-based author, native of Greenville, Alabama, residing in Houston, Texas with her husband and three beautiful children. She's a proud member of Zeta Phi Beta Sorority, Inc., The Order of Eastern Star, board member of the African American Library at the Gregory School (AALGF), and many other community efforts.

Mrs. Burrell is a former HR professional and educator who has a love for literature and working with children. As a child, she was often told that she was a great storyteller with a broad imagination. Her writings mimic her personality to uplift, engage, encourage, help you fertilize your spirit with positive thoughts, and give you reassurance of who you are. She inspires you to live a happy and fearless life of possibilities.

Made in the USA
Columbia, SC
18 April 2022